Runt the Brave

LEGENDS OF Tira-Nor BOOK ONE

THE BRAVE

bravery in the midst
of a bully society

Runt THE Brave

LEGENDS OF
Tira-Nor
BOOK
ONE

Bravery in the midst
of a Bully society

LIVING
INK
BOOKS
Writing Worth Reading

Daniel Schwabauer

First Printing—September 2012

Print edition	ISBN 13: 978-0-89957-848-4
EPUB edition	ISBN 13: 978-1-61715-367-9
Mobi edition	ISBN 13: 978-1-61715-368-6
ePDF edition	ISBN 13: 978-1-61715-369-3

THE LEGENDS OF TIRA NOR® is a trademark
of AMG Publishers

Cover layout and design by Daryle Beam at
BrightBoy Design, Inc., Chattanooga, TN

Editing by Kathy Ide and Rick Steele

Interior design and typesetting by
Adept Content Solutions LLC, Urbana, IL

Printed in the United States of America
17 16 15 14 13 12 –RO– 6 5 4 3 2 1

This book was written for
Gabrielle Joy
with love.

Really and truly.

Contents

Tamir's Prophecy

Chitter, chatter, teeth a-clatter,
Up above, an evil patter.
Tell me, mouse, what's the matter?
"We grow thin as Wroth gets fatter."

Inside, creeping, all unsleeping,
Outside, nervous vigils keeping.
Why must sorrow come a-leaping?
"Hate is deaf to helpless weeping."

Broken in a bloody maw,
Burns like fire, cuts like saw.
Turns the world on fang and claw?
"Pity those who have no law."

Close the gates and bar the door,
Cling to lamp-lit earthen floor.
Some will see the sky no more.
"Rats have come to Tira-Nor!"

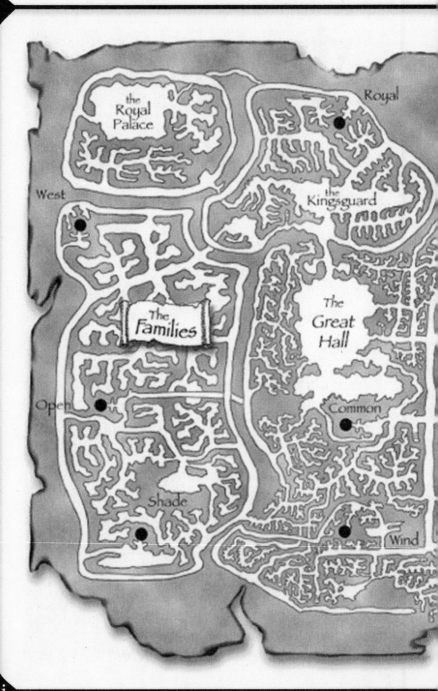

Chapter One

The Coming of Rats

At the edge of the Dark Forest, JaRed the field mouse waited for the face of death to reveal itself. An enemy lurked there under the vast canopy of oaks and maples. He felt its presence as a cold shiver along his spine.

He stood unmoving, his body stiff. A hot breeze rustled the tall prairie grass. All around him the drought-burned stalks snapped and rattled like swords. Dust choked the air, coated the leaves of weeds, rose in gentle swirls.

JaRed's nose twitched.

He blinked back the sweat that trickled down his brow and stung his eyes.

Though still young, JaRed had learned to trust the whisper of instinct. Its voice screamed at him now, raising the sweat-matted fur on the back of his neck.

He stood very still for a long time.

The mice of Tira-Nor sometimes said Death wore a different face each morning. One day it wore the face of the weasel or the cat. The next day it put on the face of the serpent. Another day it wore the pale, shriveled mask of old age. But the mice only spoke this way in macabre jest.

They knew what Death really looked like.

Death came from the sky. Its hands were talons, and its face wore a small hooked beak.

JaRed knew he should not have been scavenging near the Dark Forest in the first place. But the old familiar restlessness had overtaken him, and he had made for the shadowy black trails and shifting gloom as though drawn by the magic of its vastness. One could get lost in the Dark Forest, and sometimes "lost" appealed to him.

But now he saw something odd—something unnatural—at the forest's edge. He thought it might be important to know just what the odd thing was. For whatever enemy waited in the dry brush of the Dark Forest, it was trying hard not to be seen.

JaRed excelled at making himself disappear. This talent came easily to him, for he was smaller than the other mice—so much smaller he had been called Runt his whole life. *Runt the flea-scratcher. Runt the Sickly.*

Runt the Waste-of-Air. He had always hated these names, but what could he do? Even the older mice called him *Little Runt.*

Adults thought of him as a child simply because of his size.

At some point — he could not remember when — he had discovered that being small could be useful. When others did not respect you, they tended not to see you. This had given him an idea.

JaRed had taught himself how to move silently, how to blend into his surroundings, how to disappear virtually at will.

After a while, he could make himself almost invisible.

Perhaps this explained his overconfidence now.

The thing in the brush is not a skilled predator, he told himself, *or it would not fidget while trying to hide.*

This puzzled him.

He stepped forward lightly. Closer to the odd enemy, the death-thing. He moved like a ghost among the thistles, weeds, and long stalks of sunflowers, and stopped just inside the shadow of the Forest.

"Would you look at that," a great fist of a voice said from the gloom. "GoRec is right. A whole village of the little devils. And ripe for the plucking to boot."

"Shaddap," said a second voice. "I need to think."

JaRed froze. He stood close now, though he still could not see the enemy through the dense undergrowth. He willed his body to relax. The voices carried a tone of familiarity, something he could not quite place. But they did give Death a shape and a size, if not a face, and this blunted the edge of his fear. The most terrifying enemies had no shape or size because one never saw them. They struck before you knew they were there.

A single shock of white fur drooped just above Ja-Red's left eye, and he brushed it back with one paw. Then he nudged aside the dry yellow grass and stepped forward into the deeper cover of the Dark Forest. Under grass, between fallen twigs, around stones. Careful not to make a sound. He would not confront the voices. He would go around them. He would watch them from the thicket to the north. He would find out what sort of threat these intruders represented. But he would not be seen or heard. Of this he was certain.

"What was it Master GoRec wanted from us?" the first voice asked.

"Numbers, you dolt," replied the second. "How many mice actually live in Tira-Nor." There was a pause, then, "Anyway, must be over two thousand."

JaRed slipped forward soundlessly. He moved among the shadows, through dead grass and limp twigs and empty husks of leaves, his ears alert for every word. There were at least two of them, he knew now, but there could be more. The others might be more clever at concealing themselves.

As they continued to chatter, JaRed finally understood why they couldn't stand still. Why they betrayed their secrecy by impatience. They did not possess the ability to wait quietly for something they wanted.

They weren't predators; they were something worse.

Rats.

But what were they doing here, outside Tira-Nor?

JaRed inched forward, sure of himself now that he knew what he faced. Even so, his heart thudded in his chest. But he moved forward again, equally slowly, his body trembling. Beneath the wide tapered leaves of sunflowers that stretched their necks to drink the heat of the sky, two long, hairless tails like worms jutted from the foliage. One of the tails twisted slowly, coiling under a decaying leaf.

JaRed stood behind them, close enough to make out the brown-and-white splotches of oily fur on their backs.

"Can you smell them?" the first rat asked. Its voice sounded like a hacksaw cutting rusty tin.

"Smell them?" the other mocked. This one's voice was lower, more cumbersome, like a squash bursting under the blow of a hammer. "The stink of mice is all about this place. We shall have to do something about that when we take over. Maybe we can coax a skunk into spraying Tira-Nor down for us." The rat guffawed at its own joke, but its companion turned on it, as rats are known to do, and clapped it across the nose with one paw.

"Quiet, you idiot! Do you want to bring their sentries?"

The other sneered and continued to laugh. " What are you so afraid of, Scritch?"

Scritch looked north along the edge of the Dark Forest. His eyes narrowed into little black slits as he scanned the greenery around where JaRed stood motionless. "Do you not smell that, Klogg?"

The bigger of the two rats turned, and JaRed saw

that his face was scarred along the nose in two long, bare streaks. Klogg's nose twitched. "Mouse."

"Yes," Scritch said.

"So what? The whole area reeks of them. Weren't we just talking about—"

"No, no, no," Scritch sputtered. "Mark the direction of the wind."

Klogg paused a moment, blinking. "That way," he said at last. He raised one grimy paw and pointed north, in the direction where JaRed stood hidden.

How could I have been so stupid? JaRed thought. But there wasn't time to berate himself further. Scritch's eyes opened wide and his mouth curled back in a sly and wicked grin. His hacksaw voice scratched the air like a claw. "Yesss! There. The stink of ... a mouse!"

JaRed turned and ran. Even as he took his first desperate steps, he heard the crunching of dry grass and fallen leaves that meant the two rats were giving chase.

When threatened, a mouse of Tira-Nor would usually bolt for the cover of the closest of the city holes, which they called *gates*. Mice were fast, and most of their enemies would not risk Tira-Nor's booby traps. It was common knowledge the city's entry tunnels were well secured.

But JaRed was not close to a gate. He had been scavenging at the eastern border of the underground city's territory, which ran from the Houses of Men, past the hill they called Round Top, and all the way to the Winding Cliffs of the Dark Forest. The closest gate lay well beyond his reach now.

There was, to be sure, one gate not far from here, and though not all the mice knew of it, JaRed did. Its tunnel ran in a line all the way from the Commons of Tira-Nor to the edge of the Dark Forest near where JaRed had first spotted the rats.

But JaRed could not use it. That hole was one of the ancient defenses of Tira-Nor, to be used only in the event of dire need. It was an escape route *from* the city, not *into* it. JaRed would rather have died than reveal that secret to the rats. Tira-Nor had its faults, but it was still home, even if he did dream of escaping to a new life somewhere beyond the known world.

So he ignored the half-buried crevice in the bottle-shaped limestone that marked the hole, and instead ran through the Dark Forest. Farther from safety. Farther from home.

After what seemed a long time, he stopped, exhausted, and pushed himself under the cover of a fallen log. The bottom of the log lay just above the earth and formed a narrow cave-like crevice backed by dirt. He could not have asked for a better hiding place; the opening was much too small for a rat to shove through. He curled his tail around his heaving body, his chest pressed low to the damp ground, and sniffed at the pungent odor of rotting tree bark. He did not suppose he would have to remain hidden for long. The rats had probably given up by now and would leave him alone.

He was wrong.

◆ ◆ ◆

From his position underneath the log, JaRed stared at the fat legs and dirty paws of the two rats. With their keen sense of smell, Scritch and Klogg had followed

JaRed's trail all the way to the fallen log. Had they been in a hurry, they might have left him alone. But rats as a general rule could not resist chasing anything that runs. And JaRed had run.

Scritch lowered his head to the ground and peered into the darkness with one eye. "What have we here?"

"It's a mouse," Klogg said.

"Of course it's a mouse. But what was it doing spying on us?" Scritch spat his voice into the dark hole. "Well? What were you doing, mouse?"

"Yes," Klogg burbled. "Why were you spying on us?"

"You were the ones spying," JaRed said. "Go away."

"Go away, is it?" Klogg's scarred and bulbous nose appeared at the opening. "*We* live here now. This is our part of the forest and you're trespassing. I've a mind to give you a good beating, I do."

"Get up on the log," Scritch commanded.

Just visible beneath the black roof of the log, Klogg's eyes narrowed to half-moons. "What?"

"Get up on the log, you walking garbage heap. Jump up and down."

Klogg raised up on his hind legs, then peered again underneath the log. He raised up again and lowered himself once more. A slow, happy smile worked itself across his snout. "Ohhhhh. I see."

He leaped up on the log, and his voice came woodenly from above. "Well? Whaddaya think, mouse?" The log shuddered once, twice, as if from a great weight thundering down on it. "How does this feel, mouse? Or this? Or this?"

JaRed heard panting. But the log wasn't moving,

for it was connected to the trunk of the tree by a thick section of folded wood fiber. JaRed felt the vibrations through the fur of his back, but he still had room enough to breathe.

Scritch looked in. "Give him another go. Flatten him."

Klogg jumped and threatened some more, but his voice sounded tired.

Finally the pounding stopped.

"Let that be a lesson, mouse," Scritch growled. "No more spying on us. And if I ever catch you near Tira-Nor again, I'll feed you to Klogg one whisker at a time. That is, if you're lucky. If I'm especially angry I might introduce you to the *Master*."

◆ ◆ ◆

The oldest story any mouse could remember told of a Great Owl—as white as the moon and as silent as a shadow—that swooped for its prey from a hole in the sky. The hole was made by ElShua's finger the day he pushed the world deep into the soil of heaven, for the hole was both a window and a doorway into that other world.

According to the story, the Owl swept through the skies of ElShua's garden. He carried in his beak that trouble-making rodent, Wroth. ElShua had grown tired of Wroth causing mischief for the other animals. So he sentenced it to exile, and he gave the job of enforcing that punishment to the Owl. "Take him to the White Desert and leave him beyond the farthest dune," ElShua commanded. "There he will find no creature to torment except himself. Perhaps the loneliness of that place can remake his soul, for even Wroth must eventually tire of his own voice."

And so the Owl flew and flew. Away from ElShua's palace, over mountains, beyond rivers and valleys and plains, until he came to the edge of the great garden, the velvet fields bursting with the green hope of new worlds and new life. And all the while Wroth protested and screamed and cursed the same thing over and over: "You'll regret this!"

The Owl grew so weary of hearing his prisoner's complaints, he felt he could bear it no longer. In despair, he began to look for some way to rid himself of his burden. After all, it would be many weeks before he arrived at the White Desert, and he didn't think he could stand Wroth that long.

An idea occurred to him. The Owl saw that he flew directly over freshly turned, black-and-green fields. He saw the crisp rows, the infinitely perforated furrows like great lumps of dark bread studded with seeds. And he thought, in all this vastness surely one rodent would not make any difference. For the rows were endless, and once Wroth had been planted he would never get out.

Down the Owl flew—faster than the wind—and into a hole chosen at random, a hole made by ElShua's finger, a hole smaller than a pine needle and wider than the sun.

Inside the hole he found the newly made Earth. Newly made skies opened up around him, and below him a new sea crashed against new rocks.

"You'll regret this," Wroth shrieked again.

But the Owl opened his beak and said, "Who?"

Released from the Owl's grip, Wroth fell. He fell for three days and three nights before he hit the waves, which is why rats fear both heights and water to this very day.

But when the Owl returned to heaven he found ElShua waiting for him. And ElShua's face blazed with anger, for He did not intend His new world to suffer the presence of such evil.

"Do you know what you have done?" ElShua asked.

"Who?" said the Owl. He had never been one to accept responsibility for his deeds.

"You," said ElShua. "You have brought evil into my new world. Therefore, you will be the one to take it out. Here is your punishment: every day, for as long as the Earth blooms in my garden, you will bear its sorrow to my side."

Then they both wept, and ElShua stopped planting new worlds.

That is how the Great Owl came to be the bearer of souls.

◆ ◆ ◆

JaRed believed in ElShua. He believed in the Great Owl, though he never said so out loud. His brothers would mock him endlessly if they ever found out. Especially HaRed, whom everyone called Horrid. Horrid said it didn't really matter what you believed about life, about death.

Beneath the log, JaRed felt strangely cold. Remembering the ancient stories usually gave him a sense of warmth and peace. Instead, he felt more alone than ever.

JaRed waited all through the afternoon before he dared leave the safety of the log and begin the long journey back to the city of Tira-Nor. By then the sun had set, and the cloudless void was empty of everything but pinprick stars and the barest sliver of a moon bleeding light into the world.

People sometimes supposed field mice lived in a world of open spaces and sunshine, of wide horizons and blue sky. This was not so. The world of mice was one of darkness and shadows. To a mouse, a field of prairie tall grass was a jungle of green blades and prickly weeds. Life was secured by bolting from safety to safety, from bush to rock to tree. The sun and the moon were uncertain allies, for a mouse's eyesight during the day was inferior to that of the hawk, the badger, and the weasel. And during the night it was no match for the owl's.

Mice much preferred their underground cities, secured by a myriad of booby traps and maze-like passages, guards, roundabouts, and double-backs, as well as the comfort of shadow and the occasional convenience of phosphorescent glowstones.

JaRed loved Tira-Nor.

He also hated it.

Its network of tunnels and burrows and great-chambers were safe. Warm in winter, cool in summer, its passages welcomed JaRed with arms of earth and clay. Its history embraced him with precepts grounded in the character of the Maker. Tira-Nor was, in more than name only, "a city of promise." Tira-Nor was a city of destiny: huge and familiar and comforting. Tira-Nor was home.

But to JaRed it was suffocatingly small. For what part of the Commons hadn't he explored a thousand times? Indeed, what part of the halls of the Families — which were forbidden to mice of the Commons — had he not slipped quietly into for the sheer thrill of defiance? Sometimes the city *needed* to be defied. And sometimes a mouse needed to feel he was more than the least, more than — as Horrid had dubbed him — "half a commoner."

And yet he often wondered: did the promises of ElShua really apply to him? Did they apply to anyone? He didn't know, and not knowing troubled him.

Tira-Nor protected the bodies of its lesser citizens. But what of their souls?

JaRed arrived above the northeastern corner of the city too late to use the Mud Gate. Only two entrances to the city would be open at this hour. The gate called Open was almost always available, except when heavy rains made its steep initial plunge treacherous. The Common Gate lay protected by a lump of overhanging rock that jutted from the earth just above it. Both holes stood well to the south and east and were considerably larger, having been built by the original architects of Tira-Nor, the prairie dogs who were driven out ages ago by TyMin and the Ancients.

JaRed chose the Common Gate. He scampered inside after whistling his approach for the guard. The tunnel's smooth walls glimmered with reflected light from the moon, which stood balanced above the Dark Forest on one brilliant point.

To his surprise, Captain Blang of the kingsguard met him in the checkpoint. "Who is it?" Blang asked, sniffing at JaRed's coat.

"JaRed, son of ReDemec the Red, of the Commons."

"ReDemec has a son named JaRed?"

"Yes, sir." JaRed felt his cheeks blush. "Runt."

"Ah, yes! Now I remember."

The words stung. JaRed supposed he should not have expected someone of Captain Blang's rank to recognize him, but carrying the name *Runt* grew tiresome. Like lugging an extra tail in from the field after a long day.

Come to think of it, JaRed wondered why someone of Blang's rank should be standing gate duty.

"How is your father?" Blang asked.

"Very well, sir. I will give him your compliments."

"Do that, yes. What are you doing out so late? You've brought nothing back."

As a member of the Commons, JaRed's life and his labor belonged to the king. He was not a member of the Families, and it was his duty as a scavenger to bring back food for the storerooms.

In fact, JaRed had a single ripe mulberry stuffed in his cheek when he first felt the presence of Klogg and Scritch from a distance. But then, clumsily, he had swallowed it. He had been too startled to notice whether it even tasted good.

"Wait a moment. Runt. Yes. Someone was looking for you. Asked me to keep a whisker out. What was her name? Short and quiet. Rather cute, with a white patch on her left forepaw —"

"KahEesha," JaRed said. "My sister."

"Yes. KahEesha. Lovely thing. Asked if I would tell you to come home immediately. Something about a visitor. I can't remember the rest. Say, is she married?"

"No, sir. Thank you, sir."

"Hold on. You still haven't answered my question. What were you doing out there?"

JaRed did not want to tell Captain Blang about the rats. Not yet, anyway. The story would just condemn him to more questions and more attention. This would make his brothers angry — especially Horrid. Afterward they would make his life more miserable than it already was.

Still, he must not think of himself. It was no trivial threat he had stumbled upon. Tira-Nor must be warned.

He felt, like a cold stirring in his bones, that news of the spies must reach the king. A sense of looming danger hung over him, and he could not be rid of it.

"Captain Blang, if I tell you what happened to me, will you promise not to tell anyone but the king?"

Blang scowled. "I will make no such promise. But you *will* tell me what happened."

JaRed sighed. Blang would not understand. He did not have JaRed's brothers for family. "I suppose I must."

Blang stared at him in a suffocating silence. When he finally spoke his voice sounded like water trickling from a drain. "I am the captain of the kingsguard. I'm not going to wait forever."

"I was foraging near the Dark Forest," JaRed said, "when I came across two rats. They were spying on us, and they talked of a Master." JaRed shrugged. "I think Tira-Nor may be in danger."

"Did they hurt you?"

"No."

Blang flicked his tail and sniffed.

Jared could not tell whether Blang believed him. "May I go now?"

"One more question. Why don't you want anyone else to know what happened to you?"

"It wouldn't make sense to frighten everyone unnecessarily." Which was true enough.

"Somehow I don't think that's the reason you demanded a promise from an officer in the kingsguard."

JaRed felt his face blush again. "My brothers wouldn't like me getting a lot of attention."

Blang stared at him for another long moment. "I see."

"You won't tell them, will you?"

"No. But they may find out anyway. I believe the king will want to see you."

JaRed's stomach heaved. He could not think of anything he wanted less than to stand in front of King So-Sheth and describe his headlong flight from the two rats.

"We've known about the rats for some time now," Captain Blang said. "Which is why I'm standing gate watch for the first time in six seasons. In the next day or two a runner from the kingsguard will come for you. Don't be frightened. Just tell your story as clearly as you can. Perhaps your brothers will not find out."

"Yes, sir."

"In the meantime, give my regards to your sister, will you?"

◆ ◆ ◆

Captain Blang stood alone just inside the gate-hole and stared blankly into the night. The air tasted of dust and heat. He listened, but the only sounds he heard came from memories a lifetime past and a universe distant.

Against the black moon-washed curtain of stars, a nightmare returned. Screams of mice. Cursing. Someone shrieking as though in intense pain.

That, too, had been a dry summer, had it not?

Then the familiar smell from ages ago: the one who loved him. A gentle touch. A calm voice speaking comfort. *Shush. Be still. Father will protect us. But we must do as he says, go quickly and quietly. Can you do that? Of course you can. And Mother will come behind. The noise? It's nothing, little one. Nothing at all. Nothing to concern you. Come now, and be strong.*

Blang turned in the entrance, wondering at his own foolishness. No use thinking this way. Why go back? And yet his mind wouldn't stop, wouldn't turn to more practical matters.

He shook his head as though shaking off water after a cold swim.

Why, he wondered, were torments always born in litters? Earlier this summer the kingsguard had been decimated by an attack from two foxes—something unheard of in the history of the city. Then the drought had blown in like a hot wind from across the prairie, scorching the earth, destroying the grain, shriveling the wild berries of the Dark Forest upon which Tira-Nor depended for water. And now, the most menacing news of all: Blang's past returned. Its hollow black mouth opened like the jaws of the grave. Daily now his scouts returned grim-faced with words to make even the fiercest lose heart.

The rat army gathering to the west grew bold. They now sent spies to the very borders of Tira-Nor, where any scavenging Commoner could not fail to see them. Clearly the rat master—the one Blang's scouts referred to as *It*—meant for his rat spies to be seen. *It* wanted the people of Tira-Nor to know rats were coming. *It* wanted them to be afraid. Truly, war could not be far off.

And when war came, how would the city survive? Tira-Nor had been savaged by enemies, drought, and sickness. Its kingsguard warriors numbered fewer than two hundred. Its militia boasted barely twice that. Its stores of food were already insufficient for a mild winter, let alone an outright siege.

What would the king do?

Blang thought of the rat master, the one called GoRec, and shuddered. His scouts told of a monster too terrible for the imagination. Larger and quicker than any rat they had ever seen. And Blang knew they were not exaggerating. Such things were possible. He had seen. He had heard. Once, long ago.

The memories piled upon him, unwelcomed, but Blang was powerless to stop them.

Mother hiding him under a shiny silver rock with a hollow place, a perfect circle. Father standing up to first one, then two, then four rats. The monster appearing out of shadow and fire, its eyes like empty black pits. And Mother, her back to a wall of cinder, pleading …

He heard a low moaning sound, the wail of a frightened kit, and he realized the sound came from himself. Hot tears streaked down his cheeks. He stood alone in the night, ashamed of this terrible weakness.

Captain Blang, weeping! What would his lieutenants think?

But he could not stop, could not push the rage and helplessness beyond reach, could not crush it or whisk it away.

He knew why, just as he knew the dread he felt was not unfounded. A thought came, exploding into the present for the zillionth time: *They are not two evils, but one. The monster of my memory and the rat master GoRec are the same rat!*

But how could that be? It had happened so long ago. In a place so remote even LaRish had never heard of it.

Nausea rose in his belly, forcing him to lean against the wall for support. His legs felt suddenly and preposterously weak.

Still he wept.

The night air whispered across the prairie. A moth fluttered briefly into view and disappeared. Overhead, the night stars shivered like candles sputtering in a vast black wind. And Captain Blang stood there, not moving, simply staring into the looming darkness.

In that moment he knew. It could not be, and yet it was. The memory he'd hidden from had found him at last.

It is not rats we fight, but Lord Wroth himself. And in all of Tira-Nor, only I know what that means.

Chapter Two

The Calling of Runt

HaRed Son of ReDemec the Red was passionately lecturing his siblings — on the idiocy of forcing talented mice like himself to serve with common soldiers in the militia — when TaMir poked his white-furred face into the chamber from the tunnel.

The old fool cleared his throat. "Excuse me."

Father looked up, a stunned expression crowding his face.

"Such an honor," Mother said. "Please come in."

"Yes, yes," Father added quickly. "Come in."

An old mouse carrying the weight of many seasons, TaMir lumbered into the family's chamber, limping awkwardly on age-swollen joints.

Look at him, HaRed thought. *Puffed up with self-
importance and the king's raisins. He's proud as a bumble
bee and twice as fat!*

But then, most of Tira-Nor's citizens were proud
and fat, though no one else seemed to notice. HaRed
was constantly forced to scavenge next to mice who
were not only his physical and intellectual inferiors,
but were too stupid to realize it. As he often told himself in the field, this observation was not a matter of
pride, but of honesty. The fact that HaRed really was
smart, handsome, and athletic made pride unneces-
sary. No point in believing a lie.

"ReDemec," TaMir said, "I hope I am not intruding."

"Not at all. Just let me move this big lug of a son."
He bent over and shouted into his son's ear. "KeeRed,
wake up! We have a guest."

KeeRed, the oldest of the ReDemec children, awoke
drowsily. "That you, BeerGul?"

The twins, BeRed and MaRed, emerged from their
sleeping chambers and stood sniffing at the far corner
of the room.

"Children," Father said, "I have the honor of intro-
ducing the Seer of Tira-Nor, Master TaMir of ElShua."

A moment of uncomfortable silence passed as
TaMir looked carefully at each of them. "Are these
your sons?"

"Yes," Mother said. "Our daughter, KahEesha, is
here as well. The oldest son is KeeRed, then HaRed,
then the twins, BeRed and MaRed — we call them Berry
and Merry. And then — "

"Welcome, sir," HaRed cut in before Mother could disgrace the family by mentioning Runt's undignified existence. "We would be pleased to help you in any way."

TaMir stared at him dispassionately, and KeeRed shot him a disgusted look. HaRed didn't care. He could always twist things to his advantage. Most adults were pathetically stupid, and TaMir would be no different. All it took to control them was a little flattery, a few *sirs* and *ma'ams*, a scattered *please* and *thank you*. Do it right, and you could bite their tails one moment and have them thanking you for it the next. Wasn't that how the king treated his soldiers? Wasn't that how he treated the mice of the Commons? Give them a dark hole with their name on it and a dull job gathering nuts, and they'll follow you for life. But not HaRed. HaRed was bound for better things, and he knew it.

"I have come looking for someone," TaMir said. "ElShua sent me."

These last three words hung in the air, heavy and ominous, inspiring only silence.

HaRed wondered if the seer had come for him. Everyone knew TaMir had no apprentice. Who better than HaRed to take the position?

He turned the idea over in his mind like a rock under which he might find something of interest. The more he considered the idea, the more plausible it seemed. Was it really so unlikely that a mouse of HaRed's talents would eventually be noticed by a seer, especially if that seer was looking for a mouse of quality?

Of course, HaRed didn't really believe all that nonsense about the Ancients. The old legends and traditions were just stories for fools concocted by those in power to keep the city under control. No one with the brains of a peanut took the name ElShua seriously.

This thought gave HaRed a sense of importance, for it meant he was in the know. Others might be witless enough to believe in invisible beings, but not HaRed. He saw through the words, the formality, the bluster. He knew TaMir didn't really believe in ElShua, though the seer breathed the Name often enough. No wonder! Fear of the Name kept TaMir kept in power, protected his position as second- or third-highest mouse in the kingdom.

And now he had come to pass on that legacy!

At last, HaRed thought. *A way out of the Commons.*

"Are these *all* of your sons?" TaMir asked.

"There is another," Mother said. "He should have come home by now. His name is —"

"Runt," HaRed said quickly. He made his voice sound polite, but the word sound bad. *Runt.* The least. The smallest. *Runt the dirty. Runt the stupid. Runt the fool.* All these meanings HaRed thrust into the one syllable. The force of his spite was so strong even Mother noticed it. They all noticed it. How could they not? But when they looked at him, HaRed neither apologized nor sneered. He kept his face blank. He had said nothing wrong. Everyone called JaRed *Runt.* Just as everyone called him *Horrid.*

TaMir stared for a long time, then said, very quietly, "Perhaps I have made a mistake. But I should like to see this one called … Runt." He said the word exactly as HaRed had. Only now the similarity came as an insult. The word thudded into HaRed's dignity like an arrow striking wood.

HaRed felt his face flush. Perhaps TaMir was not as stupid as he had imagined.

"KahEesha," Mother said. "Go find JaRed. Tell him to come home right away."

◆ ◆ ◆

JaRed left Captain Blang and took the southward passage that would lead past the Wind Gate and eventually to home. The air cooled as the passage sloped downward, and when the mundane smell of dry earth filled his nostrils he felt himself relax. Sometimes he wanted to leave Tira-Nor forever, wanted it more than anything, even more than he wanted not to be small anymore. But just now the city's smooth, cool familiarity greeted him like an old friend.

KahEesha met JaRed at the second turn nearest home. The ReDemec family chambers—a comfortable space with separate sleeping holes for JaRed's parents and each of his five siblings—stood in the southwest section of the Commons some distance from the Common Gate.

"Oh, thank goodness you're back," KahEesha said, her voice too loud in the stillness. Her coat shone dully in the light of a glimmering glowstone. "Mother has been so worried. Where have you been?"

"I'll tell you later. What's wrong?"

"TaMir is waiting in our chambers. He came to Father over an hour ago, saying he was looking for a certain mouse."

"What does the Seer want?"

"Don't know for sure," she whispered. She stopped abruptly. They had been moving down the tunnel side by side, but now she turned to look at him in the near-blackness. She put one paw over his, as though in warning. "But I think he wants *you.*"

"Me?"

"I think he's come for an apprentice."

All of Tira-Nor knew the chalk-white old seer had never trained an assistant. His knowledge of ElShua's magic would die with him if he did not choose a pupil soon.

But choosing JaRed made no sense. JaRed was too small to be considered for such a high office. Besides, seers were born white. Though he did bear the single white shock of fur on his forehead, JaRed was otherwise gray as dust, and even less inspiring.

"Why would he want me?"

KahEesha shrugged. "He's examined everyone else. You're the only one left."

♦ ♦ ♦

When JaRed entered the family chamber behind KahEesha, he knew instantly something terrible was about to happen. He almost wished Scritch and Klogg had killed him back in the Dark Forest.

It's true, JaRed thought when he saw the old white mouse lurking in the corner. *He's come to make me his apprentice.*

Mother seemed glad to see him, though fear stood plainly on her face. Father's scowl betrayed his shame at JaRed's presence, as though being small were a crime as terrible as treason or murder. Brother KeeRed licked his paws in open disgust; Berry and Merry yawned with boredom; KahEesha stared breathlessly. Horrid glared at him with a look of pure malice.

"Runt," Father bellowed, his voice loud in the silence, "we have a guest."

"Yes, sir." JaRed tried to ignore the force of Father's whiplike voice snapping in the air. He willed himself taller, stronger, and fiercer, though he knew it was useless. Whenever he tried to make himself look bigger, he only succeeded in making his legs look skinny.

TaMir stirred on his haunches and shuffled closer. His white fur stood thin and flat against his body, as though even his skin were tired. Weariness gathered in the white sheet of his folded flesh. His legs wobbled on knobby joints, little stony hills that jabbed pain through his face with every step.

"You have a given name, Runt?" TaMir spoke JaRed's nickname delicately, as though it might break.

"JaRed. Sir."

"JaRed, yes." TaMir stroked his whiskers. His eyes turned upward to focus on nothing in particular, and he exhaled slowly, until JaRed began to wonder if the old mouse would ever breathe again.

Mother stepped forward, dared to place one paw on TaMir's mountainous shoulder. "Forgive me for asking, but is JaRed the one you came to see?"

TaMir looked at her and nodded. "Yes," he said, as though to himself. "He is the one."

Horrid drew a sharp breath, his face hardening into an unreadable mask.

Father glanced around the room at JaRed's brothers. "Are you sure? How can you know you haven't made a mistake?"

TaMir scowled. "Am I sure?" he snorted. "What kind of a fool's question is that? I am never sure. And mistakes? I could not recount half my blunders in a winter's telling. But I am not here on my own. I told you: ElShua sent me. And he, dear ReDemec, does *not* make mistakes."

Father recoiled from the rebuke. "Quite sure," he conceded, nodding agreeably. "Just asking."

JaRed's heart sank. He had been holding on to the thin hope that TaMir would go away without saying that JaRed was "the one." TaMir never took back his words.

JaRed's life was over. He saw it in his brother's eyes. Horrid would make his life an unending misery of fear, derision, and torment. All because JaRed had achieved, without even trying, an honor the others could not possibly have wanted. An honor JaRed didn't want himself.

JaRed felt the unfairness of everything rising to swallow him whole. Red would hate him, and Merry and Berry would hate him. Horrid, who already hated him, would hate him even worse. And Father would hate him for humiliating his family.

Unless. A thought leapt into JaRed's mind, bearing with it a tiny seed of hope. *Unless being apprenticed to TaMir is such a lofty position even Horrid would not dare to touch me.*

Was such a thing possible? Was there really a safe place in the universe after all? A place where neither Horrid nor the Great Owl dared to go?

The old seer shuffled closer to JaRed. "You have always been considered according to your size, haven't you? But there is one who does not judge by outward things, by great strength or an oiled coat or a quick leap. You have been chosen from all of Tira-Nor, from all the world. ElShua's breath is on you."

TaMir's breath was on him as well, for the old mouse now stood so close to JaRed their noses touched. The seer's fur smelled of damp earth, and his short yellow teeth jutted from his mouth like kernels of dried corn. But JaRed did not fear him. Rather, he felt a strange sense of awe. TaMir exuded a kind of surging gentleness. This was not at all what JaRed had expected from a legendary prophet. On the contrary, TaMir seemed ... *nice.*

"Listen to my words." TaMir knelt, wincing as he bowed his great weight, and gathered one of the Ja-Red's paws into his own. "You have been appointed by the Maker of tails and teeth, by the bringer of snow and song, by the source of wind and wisdom, to be a fang for his venom and a feast in the house of famine. You will pluck his enemies from the grass with a crushing beak. You will summon the talons of the Great Owl."

JaRed listened with a growing sense of fear and anticipation. *Could it really be true?*

Only Mother seemed glad. "Oh, please, Master TaMir. Didn't you always speak in riddles? I must know. Have you come to take my little JaRed away?" Her words spilled out all at once, like grain from a broken jar. "I always knew he was special. But when will you take him as your apprentice? Is it to be now? Or is there a coming of age?"

JaRed closed his eyes, fighting back anger. *My little JaRed?* He wanted to scream. *Why must I always be thought of as little?*

TaMir looked up. "Apprentice? I said nothing about taking an apprentice."

The hope in JaRed's heart died instantly. *I should have known it was too good to be true.*

Horrid's face registered surprise and exultation.

"Isn't that what you've come for?" Father asked. "To choose an apprentice?"

TaMir shook his head. "I told you. I do not do the choosing. I have come for one reason only: to announce ElShua's decision." He turned back to JaRed. "Have you not understood?" His voice flowed through the room like sand, stretching out to all of them. "JaRed, you are the next king of Tira-Nor."

TaMir's words hung in the air like smoke: majestic, heavy, suffocating.

"We already have a king," Horrid whispered through clenched teeth. He crouched in the corner like a coiled serpent, and JaRed knew with gut-shredding certainty that Horrid would find a way to turn TaMir's words into trouble.

"I did not say JaRed would *usurp* King SoSheth," TaMir said. "Only that he would *succeed* him."

But JaRed knew what they were all thinking, because he was thinking the same thing. *This is treason. King SoSheth has a son. Won't Prince JoHanan have something to say about who takes the throne after his father?*

Horrid's eyes glittered like tiny jewels.

"I can't be king," JaRed said. "I'm not even strong."

TaMir looked through him, behind him, at nothing. "He will hate you for what I have done. But the words are not mine." His voice was as quiet as a dragonfly's wings beating the air. For just a moment the room filled with warmth and peace and majesty, as though some-one of immense power had entered and was watching, listening.

"It is not might that makes right, in spite of what people say. It is right that makes might."

◆ ◆ ◆

The mice of Tira-Nor tell a story about those first months on Earth after Wroth came dripping from the waves. It is said the first mice, the Mice of the Sea Caves, took pity on him and brought him back to their communal home beneath the cliffs.

At first they did not know what to make of Wroth. For one thing, he was twice the size of the biggest among them. For another thing, his tail was completely bald. For a third thing, his nose shot as long and sharp as a needle from his forehead.

Some said he was not a mouse at all, that he was some different sort of creature. But others pointed to the obvious similarities between Wroth and themselves.

And so the Sea Cave Mice took pity on Wroth and tried to nurse him back to health. They gave him the best cave to sleep in. They brought him strawberries and nuts and sunflower seeds, though after the first berry he never ate any more. They oiled and perfumed his fur as he lay still in the center of his cave.

They decided, eventually, that he must be suffering some kind of delirium. For day and night he shrieked the same thing over and over: "You'll regret this!"

Portending doom rhythmically, like a siren. Hour after hour.

"You'll regret this!"

The Sea Cave Mice had never encountered evil, so they did not know the meaning of the word *regret*. Nor did they recognize Wroth's wicked heart for the black and empty thing it was.

They did not even know a heart *could* be black and empty, for their hearts were still mostly the way ElShua had made them.

Mostly. Though the Voice had already begun to work its destruction.

They assumed Wroth merely lay ill, and they tried harder and harder to help him. They brought him more food, all of which went uneaten. They left it in piles in his cave, afraid to linger there. Wroth's body began to waste away, until his ribs poked grimly through his oily skin and his eyes bulged in their sockets like empty wells.

Wroth did not sleep. And, strangely, he did not get hoarse. If anything, his voice grew louder. It boomed through the caves like a thunderclap. It stabbed into the ears of the Sea Cave Mice when they rested and when they worked. It twisted their dreams and shattered their morning-songs. It scratched the life out of every lullaby.

A few of the Sea Cave Mice slipped way in darkness, without saying good-bye. These became the Inland Mice, the ancestors of the mice of Earth.

But such desertion took great courage, and not many made it safely to the warm fields and bright sunshine. For just as a mouse had worked up the courage to run — perhaps even as he or she slipped through the darkness of night to the moonlit shore — the voice of Wroth would come poisonously from above.

"You'll regret this!"

Then a mouse would probably stop. For who knew? The Voice seemed to be speaking to just that one mouse in the whole world. And the Voice wanted the mouse to stop and come back.

By then of course the word "regret" had indeed taken on both sound and meaning.

Wroth's voice had become a knife, ripping apart their souls. Every word stung like a lash.

Until at last their minds were as dead and barren as sand, and all anyone ever thought about was the sound of Wroth's screaming.

◆ ◆ ◆

HaRed did not sleep that night. He lay curled into a ball in his sleeping chamber and stared through the opening at the ghost-blue haze of a glowstone misting the outer tunnel. Occasionally he flicked his tongue across the dry flesh of his lips, but for the most part he lay very still and thought of ways to murder Runt.

He could not kill the little flea-scratcher himself. He must find someone else to do it.

Rage, hot and dry as the summer dust, smoldered in his chest. If there had ever been any doubt Runt was Mother's favorite, that doubt was gone. What was it she had said? *I always knew he was special.*

The words sizzled and popped in his memory like grease spattering hot coals. *My little JaRed.* Her voice twisted in his mind, jeering him. She was so pleased with her favorite son. And HaRed? HaRed was just another whisker in the portal.

Father's favorite had always been KeeRed because he was the eldest. Merry and Berry favored each other, as twins usually do. But how was it possible Mother had loved the smaller son, the weakling, over the stronger one?

Mother despised HaRed's ambition. His aggressiveness. His intelligence. At least she'd finally admitted it.

His tongue spread a thin line of spittle across his teeth. Runt was nothing. A festering boil. A piece of dung. *Yet they would make him greater than me!*

HaRed slid from his chamber and crept catlike into the larger room. Fury animated his limbs, kept his tail straight. He nosed into JaRed's sleeping hole and was surprised to find the little waste-of-air awake.

HaRed pressed his face near JaRed's ear. "Runt," he hissed. "Special," he mocked. His words flowed cool and smooth as silver. "Do not forget who you are, Runt. King SoSheth will hear of your treason. And then rats will eat Mother's precious little Runt for supper!"

Chapter Three

Before the King

JaRed did not sleep during the slow night that followed the seer's proclamation. Horrid's words burned a hole through his heart, leaving a black tunnel of fear.

In the morning a runner from the palace brought a message from King SoSheth: JaRed was to appear before the king in the Royal Hall at noon.

After the runner left, the ReDemec family said nothing to him, but JaRed knew what they were thinking. *Could TaMir have been right?*

JaRed's heart pounded so fiercely he thought everyone must hear it. Had Horrid already made good his
threat to report JaRed as a traitor?

The morning stretched into eternity, made worse
by the fact that neither he nor Horrid nor any of his
brothers had drawn foraging duty. The silent persecu-
tion turned into vicious taunting as noon approached.

"If it isn't King Runt," KeeRed said, poking his face
into JaRed's chamber. "What will his highness have for
tea today?"

"Yes, Majesty," Horrid said. "Wouldst thou like
some royal grain to give thee size?"

"Or raisins from thy storehouse?" BeRed said.

"Or peanut cream?" added MaRed.

And so it went. *Do this, Runt. Do that, Runt. Hurry
up, little brother Runt. That is, if it doesn't tax thy royal
strength!*

At last JaRed slipped away and headed through
the Commons and past the outer chambers of the
Great Hall to the section of Tira-Nor that housed the
kingsguard.

Here the entrance tunnel sloped downward
through hardened clay that glimmered red in the light
of wall-mounted glowstones, so that JaRed seemed to
be passing through a shimmering red throat until he
came to the public entrance to the palace.

A dark mouse of the kingsguard greeted him.
"What's your business?"

"I'm to see the king," JaRed said. "He sent for me."

"Sent for you?" The guard eyed him suspiciously,
then turned back toward the guard room. "LaRish?"

An older mouse poked his head into the chamber.

He wore the lean, hard look of a fighter, but stared at JaRed with eyes that betrayed a sense of humor. "What is it now, CorKer?" His accent made the name sound like *Corkair*.

As a kit, JaRed had heard stories of LaRish coming to Tira-Nor from far away and turning the tide in the battle of Cliff's Edge. Of LaRish single-handedly covering the kingsguard's retreat on the Day of The Cat. Of LaRish vanquishing the three champions of Renna.

CorKer nodded toward JaRed. "You know anything about a commoner come to see the king?"

"I don't know anything about anything. I am out of favor this week."

CorKer turned back to JaRed. "No one said anything to us when we came on duty."

"I was told to report here at noon," JaRed said. "Captain Blang's orders."

At the mention of Captain Blang, CorKer twitched his nose, like a dog sniffing for trouble. "Captain Blang. Yes. I see."

LaRish rolled his eyes. "Can you not tell that this one, he is not lying? Do you not see his eyes, *Corkair*?"

"I see only his breeding."

LaRish snorted. "Bah! I will take him to the Royal Hall myself."

CorKer raised one eyebrow. "But the king said —"

"What is the worst he could do to me, eh? Have me *keeled*? At my age it would not be so great a loss. Besides, he will maybe pat me on the back and congratulate me for my good sense." He turned his attention to JaRed. "Come ... what is your name?"

JaRed liked this LaRish. And he wanted LaRish to like him. "I am JaRed. Son of ReDemec the Red."

LaRish thought for a moment. "They call you Runt, yes? Meaning *the small one,* I think." He stroked his chin. "This a good name. Sometimes small can be dangerous, like the point of a claw. And sometimes a small thing can be underestimated, which is good for the small thing. Come with me."

They wound through the lavish perimeter tunnel of the kingsguard level of Tira-Nor, which was lit by glowstones at every turn. Beyond another checkpoint the passage dipped and plunged downward, and the air grew cooler. Light fairly blazed from the corridors ahead.

Some of these glowstones could be put to better use in the Commons, JaRed thought, though he didn't say so out loud.

Outside the Royal Hall they stopped in an antechamber. "Wait here," LaRish said. He went through the entry into the Royal Hall. When he returned he said, "The king will see you when he feels like it. Right now he is blabbing to Master TaMir, the looker."

"The looker?" JaRed asked. "You mean the seer?"

"Seer, looker, whatever. Titles are not important. Only what you do, yes?"

LaRish rose up on two legs and leaned his back against the rounded wall of the antechamber. His legs flexed as he scratched his back against the rough texture of the dried mud. "Ah! this is good! Not so good as the royal scratching stones of Frevoirzheis ... but not so bad as the dungeons of BarraKog. Would you like to try?"

JaRed shook his head.

"Maybe you are too young to need itching. Wait until you are older. I think then you will itch plenty."

"Will it be a long time?" JaRed asked.

"Don't know. I started itching when I was a kit."

"I meant, will it be a long time before the king sees me?"

"Long, short, who knows? The king can blab like crazy, except when he doesn't want the talk. Then he make everyone be quiet like snails." LaRish leaned forward. "There is something I must tell you. Remember this when you speak to him. The king is not one mouse but two."

JaRed cocked his head to one side. "What do you mean?"

"Tira-Nor, it has two kings. One who is wise and calm and another who is angry and foolish. But they only have one crown and one head. The problem is, you never know when you go to see King SoSheth which one you will meet."

"You're saying he is unpredictable?"

LaRish clapped his front paws together. "That is the word. And now you know what is the problem with the king, you know what is the problem with LaRish too. I do not have good control of the tongue. When the king says something stupid, I say, 'Hey, king, that was stupid!' And then the king gets mad and tells me he is going to *keel* me and make me a *corporale* and I have to sleep in the guard room. But when the other king comes back and remembers I am a good friend to the king and to Tira-Nor, the good king says, 'Why are you sleeping in the guard room? Come back into the palace.' And he promotes me to *generale* again. So that is my problem. I never know where I will be sleeping."

LaRish poked his head into the Great Hall and looked back to JaRed. "I think the king is almost done blabbing to Master TaMir. This is a good time to go in."

◆ ◆ ◆

JaRed followed LaRish into the vast hall of the king, which was second in size only to the Great Hall that stood like a vast black void between the endless chambers of the Commons and the tight quarters of the kingsguard.

As LaRish approached, King SoSheth stopped speaking. TaMir, standing to king's left, drew back into the shadows.

LaRish stood at attention. "The king has sent for JaRed son of ReDemec, the one who is called Runt."

"Yes, yes, I'll see him." The king waved dismissively. "What is it, mouse?"

JaRed looked around, bewildered. "You sent for me, Majesty."

King SoSheth scowled. "Captain Blang has informed me that you met two rat spies yesterday. Tell me what happened."

JaRed sighed, relieved that this summons had nothing to do with TaMir's visit. He poured out his story. The words flowed in a long stream, without interruption.

Afterward, King SoSheth nodded. "Another sighting. They have crossed our borders in daylight."

TaMir stepped forward. "It is an act of war, my king. It cannot be long before they attack."

"How many times must I say it? We cannot afford a war with the rats!"

"Which is undoubtedly why they talk as though the city is already theirs. We must prepare for a siege, Majesty."

SoSheth shook his head. "We haven't the strength for a prolonged conflict. The kingsguard was depleted by last year's plague, and the militia will hardly be capable of mounting a prolonged defense. And after this drought, what will we do for water?"

"We have no other choice."

"No?" SoSheth stared into the darkness at the edge of the chamber. "What about the long hall?"

TaMir scowled. "The escape tunnel? You must not even consider it, Majesty." His voice echoed ominously in the silence that followed.

JaRed agreed, though he didn't say so. The Dark Forest was no place for females and kits.

"Why not?" SoSheth's teeth ground together, as though to crush the word *not* into powder.

"We haven't the strength to guard the helpless once we are out in the open. We will lose too many. With the defenses of Tira-Nor intact, we can force the rats to fight in unfamiliar territory, in *our* territory."

"Enough!" King SoSheth slammed one paw against the dirt floor of the hall. "I will hear no more about it."

TaMir limped forward. "As you wish. But there is a defense you haven't considered."

"Pray, enlighten me."

"ElShua will not abandon us in a time of dire need. He will send help."

"ElShua," SoSheth growled. "What will he do? Cause the rats to fall over dead outside our gates?

Kill them in their sleep? Or will he stuff our storage chambers with fresh berries and wild seed while we teach our kits about TyMin and the Ancients? If ElShua wanted to help us, he could start by making it rain. I need real help, not fantasies."

"Fantasies?" TaMir repeated softly.

"Hoping for help from ElShua is like hoping for rain. The more you need it, the less you will get."

JaRed stepped forward. "Your Highness," he blurted. "ElShua is not a liar." Even as the words spilled out, he understood his great foolishness. One did not speak freely with the king as one spoke to a commoner.

LaRish cleared his throat.

The king turned, his eyes filled with fire. "Why are *you* still here?" He pointed toward the entryway and snarled. "Get out!"

I have made another enemy, JaRed thought as he retreated from the palace. But even the king should not speak against ElShua. Especially the king. For *no Elshua* meant *no hope.*

◆ ◆ ◆

They say the voice of Wroth stopped as abruptly as a spring rain.

They also say the Mice of the Curse did not notice at first. And when they did notice, they pretended not to. For what if hope should be shattered? What if the voice returned?

But two days passed, and someone gathered courage. A mouse peered into Wroth's chamber.

Wroth was not there. The nuts, seeds, and moldering berries still stood in random piles. The room still reeked of oil. And in the center, a round dimple cratered the dirt where his body had curled in its restless inactivity. In the center of the dimple lay a single, ripe strawberry.

But no body. No hairless tail. No withering gaze.

The Inland Mice understood this only much later. The Mice of the Curse never understood it.

Wroth the Twisted had eaten one strawberry, that first offering of the Mice. And in return the strawberry's poison had eaten him.

Wroth had taken what he pleased from ElShua's gardens for so long, the obvious never occurred to him. He had not realized that Earth's fruit might be different, that it was not made for him, just as he had not been made for it.

The strawberry destroyed him. Its ripe juices ate away at his organs like an acid, burning within him night and day, hour after hour. It scoured his belly and devoured his bones.

Within moments of swallowing it, his body began to spasm. By the second day he could not move at all. He lay curled into a tight husk of rotting flesh, his eyes popping out even as his skin drew inward.

And yet his voice never failed.

The Inland Mice understood this, too. Wroth's voice issued not from mouth, lungs, and vocal chords, but from a tormented soul, from a disembodied spirit condemned to walk between—yet never in—the realms of heaven and Earth.

When the voice at last did stop, the Mice of the Curse stood in a group outside Wroth's chamber, their eyes darting from floor to ceiling to center. Could it be true? Freedom? Sunshine? *Silence*?

Hope, dazzling in its newness, appeared among them. At last, Wroth was gone.

There was a moment. A time between possibilities. A pause long enough for a hundred conflicting thoughts, until even the most timid gathered the nerve to chirrup a sigh of relief and open the door of longing in a mouse's heart.

Somehow Wroth knew. This was the perfect moment.

He spoke again, his voice cracking like the ice of a mighty river under thaw.

"You'll regret this!"

Then came the bodiless laughter, high and sudden and furious, crashing outward like a gale from the very center of the dimple.

◆ ◆ ◆

JaRed stood alone at the opening of the Wind Gate and stared west into the brown stalks of tall prairie grass that whispered and shook in the face of a dry, stiff breeze.

He had come to this place to think, to put together all that had happened in the last two days. And to escape the jealousy of his brothers.

His audience with the king had shaken him. *Did King SoSheth not believe?*

Then why all the pretense, the extravagant offerings, the annual fasts and long prayers? Why repeat the old stories about the Ancients and their legendary miracles? Why teach youngsters something he thought untrue?

Stranger still, why *didn't* the king believe? What did SoSheth know that he hid from his people?

JaRed stared motionless into the cloudy gloom of dusk. The world seemed a cold and lonely place, as though life itself had become, in an afternoon, meaningless.

But the world was not empty.

A shadow swept into the plains of Tira-Nor like some mythical beast. Something worse than drought. Worse than predators.

Something to shake one's convictions to the very core.

JaRed felt the presence of an evil larger than anything he could imagine lurking just beyond the grass. He wondered what face it would wear when it finally showed itself.

Perhaps it stood as close as Round Top, and was even now staring back at him with hungry, blood-filled eyes.

Perhaps, he thought, *it is Lord Wroth himself.*

Chapter Four

Black in the Tunnel

In the black of night a great serpent slid into Tira-Nor, its movements as silent as death.

JaRed saw the thing gliding like a dark ghost through the murky tunnels of his imagination. In his dream he understood the snake hunted not him alone, but all of Tira-Nor.

He sat under the vaporous canopy of the Royal Hall. TaMir knelt there, as did Father, Red, Horrid, and KahEesha. They were kneeling to him.

He looked for Mother, but she was not there. He felt like a kit again, unabashedly seeking her comfort, and disappointed that she was not there to see him crowned.

Then, in an instant, they were all gone, and the serpent hovered in the blackness above him. "You? A king?" It laughed. "You are a runt! More a morsel than a meal. Hold still while I eat you. Hold still while I eat your people."

JaRed's skin trembled. Fear and anger battled within his soul.

Something else slid into the room. Something good, but also terrifying. Though he could not see it, he felt it as surely as he felt the beads of sweat coursing through his fur.

Outside, high above the still, silent earth, a dark silhouette blotted the half-disk of the moon. JaRed recognized the shape at once. It was the Great Owl, vast and dark and ominous, sweeping the sky with outstretched wings, descending in a soundless spiral to the plain of Tira-Nor.

Down and down the Owl came until it was a shadow on the corn, stretching long and thin and deadly on the grass. At the eastern edge of the plain it swooped into the bottle-shaped rock and was swallowed into the crevice concealed there.

The things JaRed saw seemed both real and unreal. He watched himself rise and move from his sleeping hole into the family chamber, and from there into the tunnel outside. He padded east, toward the escape tunnel at the perimeter of Tira-Nor.

For a moment after he came fully awake, he didn't understand how far he had walked. Then he saw the dark hole into the escape tunnel, and he stood there in the dim light of a glowstone, marveling.

Had it, after all, been anything but a strange dream? Had he walked all this way in his sleep?

He ought to go back. He had foraging duty tomorrow. He would need his rest.

His skin trembled. The *something* he had felt when TaMir touched him filled the tunnel with its unseen presence, turning JaRed's stomach to water. He *had* to go on. Something terrible would happen if he didn't.

He was not sure that something terrible wouldn't happen anyway. But there was no way around it. The presence compelled him.

He stepped into the circle of darkness. Though he grew more terrified with each step, part of him actually liked the feeling. He felt as though he had found a purpose, something for which he was created. Not merely to survive such paralyzing fear, but to go beyond it— to feel the horror and take those impossible steps into darkness anyway.

He came to the guard chamber that marked the underground gate of Tira-Nor. A fading glowstone cast ghostly shadows limed in a green haze down the length of the hollow labyrinth ahead. The tunnel stretched out before him like an open mouth.

The old sentry at the guard chamber lay asleep at his post, but sputtered awake as JaRed nosed into the room. "Eh? Who is it? Well, speak up!"

"Hello, GrouSer," JaRed said, relieved to see a familiar face. He had known GrouSer since childhood.

"That you, little JaRed? Eyesight ain't what it used to be, bless my soul." GrouSer's drooping gray whiskers sprouted from his nose in wiry hoops, like straw shagging the end of an old broom. One of these had twisted around itself like a coiled spring and stuck fast in the end of GrouSer's nose. GrouSer smoothed it back with one paw, his eyebrows stitched into a semi-permanent scowl. The order that resulted from his smoothing lasted perhaps three seconds before the offending whisker recoiled stubbornly back into his nose.

"Confound it!" GrouSer muttered, smoothing the whisker back again. "I've a mind to gnaw it off. What are you doing down here at this infernal hour?"

"I had a ... well, a nightmare, I guess. Just walking it off."

"Well, don't go too far. I don't fancy coming after you."

The tunnel wound deep into the earth. At its belly a shallow pool of cold water had collected. Jared would have to wade through it in order to go on. He paused and sniffed. The water smelled of clay and algae. He lapped a mouthful, but spat it out again. The bitter aftertaste of sulfur clung to his teeth.

This would be Tira-Nor's last hope of moisture in the event of attack. Enough water for perhaps a hundred mice. Enough for a few days at most, and they would be desperate indeed before they drank it.

He shoved the thought aside and stepped into the cool water.

When he reached the end of the pool, he shook out his fur and trudged on. The tunnel rose and twisted, and JaRed passed the numerous switchbacks, double-turns, pits, hooks, and fool's errands that ensured the route's safety. He knew by heart the way through the tunnel, whispered to him by his mother from the day of his birth in the sing-song poetry of tradition.

Quick is the hunter, and quick the prey.
Quick is the sun at end of day.
Quick to hear and slow to say,
Slower still when you've lost your way.
Better to wait in long delay
Than end in stillness, death, decay.

JaRed knew the meaning, of course. The first tunnel was the *hunter*, the second *prey*. The fourth tunnel led to a maze of confusing, almost unending, identical passages and fool's errands. The last ended in a sudden deep pit studded with spikes. JaRed took the third tunnel on the right.

At last he came to the end hall, the hall of the Rock and Pillar. It was also called by an even older name, but that name sent a shiver of fear down his spine. A glowstone illuminated the chamber.

He shuffled forward and stood in the center of the yawning space that had once been called the Chamber of Wroth.

Built by the ancient prairie dogs as a hall of worship, the room was floored and roofed by two enormous slabs of limestone.

Long ago, the roof rock had begun to settle inward, and the Ancients had placed a supporting pillar at the north end to keep the rock from collapsing. When the mice of Tira-Nor decided to use the tunnel as an escape route, they gnawed through the pillar until only a narrow portion remained in the center. Now the pillar was shaped like an hourglass.

The mice of Tira-Nor may have lacked other qualities, but they were magnificent architects of dirt and wood. They knew when to stop gnawing. The roof rock balanced on little more than a bare twig now, yet it was said the roof had not moved a hair since the dedication of the tunnel.

On the north side of the chamber and extending from the beam itself, the mice had erected a thin wall of caked mud that joined the exit on the east side. The wall created the illusion of continuing tunnel to anyone coming from the other direction. In retreat, one brave mouse could stay behind and collapse the tunnel by gnawing through the beam. But an enemy coming from the opposite side would not know the beam was even there.

All this JaRed knew, for many stories were woven around this ancient bloody chamber. But now JaRed saw something more. He understood why the Ancients had been driven out of this place so long ago. He saw the thing that had brought an anger so large the ground trembled with it.

In the pillar the Ancients had carved a wild and terrifying statue of Lord Wroth. The tunnel mice had plastered over the pillar with mud, but the mud had caked and fallen away, revealing Wroth's sneering face like something out of a nightmare.

Wroth's wooden mouth hung open. Between his teeth the mutilated body of a mouse dangled lifelessly.

JaRed stared.

Wroth seemed to stare back.

Why, JaRed wondered, would anyone worship such a malevolent god, a god of double-dealings and lies, a god of hunger and pain?

Every mouse knew *that* story.

◆ ◆ ◆

Wroth owned the mice afterward, yet his lust for vengeance knew no bounds.

The Mice of the Curse had suffered mightily, for the Voice had stolen both work and work's rewards. It had stolen their play and the fruit of playing.

Under this torment their bodies changed. They slouched. They looked always down, never up. They muttered and licked their lips, as though to glean crumbs from a past meal.

They hungered.

Now Wroth used new words. He allowed a faint promise of goodness to edge his voice. He spoke of a bright and promising future. A not-too-distant Might Be. Days of Much.

He summoned a council on the night of a full moon and commanded a mouse be chosen by lot.

The mice obeyed. A mouse was chosen.

It huddled before the dimple in the cave, trembling.

Wroth offered the others a bargain. In exchange for one *tiny, eensy-weensy* little favor, he would make them great. He would give them tremendous size and strength to crush their enemies. He promised they would never hunger again. He promised them a glorious future!

And all he asked was this one insignificant nothing. A trifling hardly worth the breath of mention.

"Kill this mouse!" Wroth said quietly.

The chosen mouse shivered.

The others huddled in silence. The air in the cave grew heavy. Not so much as a nose twitched.

It was said that this was the turning point of the beginning of the world. If the mice were to become good and free again, this would have been the time and place to have done it. But the brave ones had already fled.

And so there was only silence. Until at last one mouse found the courage to ask, "What does *kill* mean?"

Afterward, when the deed was done and blood stained their paws, the Earth trembled so violently the sea rose up against the cliffs nearly to the mouth of the caves. The sun hid its face. The stars blinked into darkness for grief.

The mice shut their eyes against the agony of the universe. Against the twisting nausea that coursed through their bodies. Against wave after wave of hopelessness.

When the mice opened their eyes again they understood all at once. Behold! The black magic of the netherworld had worked! Wroth had made them huge and strong. New muscles stretched beneath oily fur. New fat padded their bellies. And yet ...

What was this? What had happened to their tails? What had happened to their dignity? Where, by thunder, was the hair?

But Wroth had fulfilled his promise that they would never hunger. Wasn't the chamber filled with food? Didn't it contain all that those first terrified servants of Wroth could hope to eat? The stuff stood in piles around the cave. Mushy berries. Fuzzy nuts. Dripping greens.

Wroth had given them an appetite for garbage, for rottenness, for decay. He had remade his slaves into his own image. No longer would they be called *mice*. Now they would be called "little Wroths," which, in the diminutive, was pronounced "raths."

They were *rats*. Now and forever.

The voice came again, echoing its high, horrible, mocking laughter: "You'll regret this!"

As the first rats stared in horror at their naked tails. As they gazed at one another in sudden understanding. As the first irresistible cravings for garbage began to grip them.

♦ ♦ ♦

JaRed had come to this hall to do something important. He had to go on.

He felt the presence again. And though the whisper of common sense that had been telling him to go back still screamed in his heart, it sounded hollow now.

Just beyond Wroth's chamber, he stopped abruptly. A shape like a smear of black ink loomed ahead of him in the darkness of the tunnel. He recognized its death smell instantly. And just as instantly, he knew the shape saw him.

"Little one," the snake said. "Why do you tremble ssso?" Its tongue flicked out in a silent stream. "Are you frightened?"

It was a king snake that loomed before him in the darkness. A female, by the gentle lilt of her voice.

"I saw you coming," JaRed said.

"Sssaw me?" Curiosity edged her voice.

"In a dream. I thought you were an omen. Or a symbol. But now I see you are real."

"Yesss. Real as hunger."

"Have you a name?"

"I am called Black, little one. And you?"

He thought about that for a moment. "I am called Runt."

"Ah, yesss. Because you are ssso sssmall. No more than a morsel, really. A sssnack. Not a meal." As Black spoke she came closer, not as snakes move in an open field, for there wasn't room for her to move quickly. She came inch by inch, her side-to-side motion constrained in the narrow tunnel.

JaRed took a step back. "No, I am not a meal. But I know where you can find one." He paused. "If you are willing."

She stopped moving. "Why should I bargain with a moussse?"

"Because this tunnel is booby–trapped."

"I can get past your puny traps without your help." Black's voice rang with self-confidence. "I found *you*, didn't I?"

"No, I found you. And I saw the Great Owl go before you."

Her tongue flicked out again, and JaRed wondered if mentioning the Great Owl had been a mistake. Owls were as much an enemy of the snake as of the mouse.

"I'm lissstening."

JaRed took a deep breath, his heart pounding like a clenched fist. "My enemies inside Tira-Nor can be your supper."

"Your life for theirs?"

"Yes."

Black edged closer. "What's to prevent me from dining on you now?"

He took two steps backward. "You are slow in the tunnel. You haven't the space to move quickly. And I know where the passages narrow, where they fall into dead-ends and pits from which you will not be able to escape."

She stopped and considered. "What are your terms?"

JaRed crouched low in the darkness. He thought of home, and realized that in spite of everything he loved his family. The thought bore with it an idea. "I know a chamber with seven fat mice sleeping soundly. I will pass by it, but I will not enter it. Follow me, but do not come too close or I will run and sound the alarm."

She flicked her tongue. "You will guide me through the tunnel if I promise to eat your seven fat friends instead of you?"

"But you must eat *only* the seven." She could probably live for months with seven mice in her belly, but what would prevent her from curling up in the Great Hall forever? "And you must promise to leave Tira-Nor afterward."

She didn't answer for a long time. JaRed knew her answer would be a lie, but the snake was clever. She seemed reluctant to offer such a promise, as though she considered her word binding.

"You asssk no trifling thing," Black said at last. "But for seven swallows I will make that promissse."

"Say it," JaRed insisted.

Her tongue flicked out. "Very well. I promissse to leave after I am finished eating."

This was just the sort of deception JaRed expected. She had promised to leave when she was finished eating, not after she'd eaten the seven. If his plan didn't work, she would not be "finished" until she devoured all of Tira-Nor.

JaRed forced himself to smile and slipped away.

Black the snake followed.

◆ ◆ ◆

When JaRed came to the false wall at the north end of the Chamber of Wroth, he scurried into the room and waited at the far end. Black's enormous face came soon afterward, filling the space between the gnawed column and the real wall.

"The tunnel narrows here, just before it opens into this worship chamber," JaRed said.

Black pushed forward, but there wasn't enough space for her to pass. The wide spade of her jaws stuck fast between the column and the wall.

"You will have to push. The tunnel widens here where I am."

Black pushed. As she did, the pillar bowed outward. JaRed imagined the roof shifting above him, and he knew there were only two possibilities once the snake had broken the beam. Either the roof would collapse and kill them both, or it would not collapse at all, and he would be left facing her wrath.

"Little one, have you betrayed me?" The pillar bulged as Black strained through the space between her and the wall. "It will not go well with you if you have."

"What do you mean?"

She stopped thrusting forward. "I can smell you. And I can smell air moving. There is another opening into this chamber. Do not think you have outwitted me today. I will find you when I come back."

She tried to back out, not knowing how close the other way into the chamber was. JaRed could see the crack in the false wall that was letting air circulate faintly through the room.

She wouldn't take long to figure out the trick. When she followed the air to the crack and pressed against the false wall, JaRed would be doomed. She would push through the thin strip of mud on the other side of the column and there would be nothing to stop her from eating all of Tira-Nor.

JaRed felt a sense of hopelessness, the same feeling that had struck him when King SoSheth said ElShua was a mere fantasy. But the old stories were true, weren't they? Good and evil weren't just ideas. They were real. Doing the right thing mattered, and the old promises of the city mattered, and the reality of the one who made the promises mattered.

Or was JaRed just hiding from the awful truth that Tira-Nor and its mice stood alone in an evil world? The truth that JaRed, *Runt*, stood alone now in an indifferent city?

What if the only other presence in this black and bloody room was the one seeking his destruction?

Wroth's statue sneered at him. The spiked jaws seemed to close; the mouse in his teeth seemed to twitch.

JaRed flung these thoughts from his mind and stepped closer to the pillar. "I'm right here. What are you so afraid of?"

"Afraid? Of a mouse?"

"Well, you were taking so long, I wondered if perhaps you were giving up. You wouldn't be the first of the great enemies to decide it was hopeless to attack Tira-Nor."

"Hopeless? I will show you hopeless." Her face appeared in the opening, her mouth stretching into a sneer as she pushed.

JaRed stepped back, turning his face away from the fetid air that blasted from her nostrils. Pieces of the false wall crumbled as her heaving sides strained outward. "I knew you weren't strong enough. I should have found a bigger snake."

Black cursed JaRed, his family, and mice in general. She fumed and threatened. Strong enough! She would show him strong enough!

He thought of TaMir's stories in the Great Hall, remembered the old seer's face in the center of a crowd of awe-struck kits. "If you ever encounter an angry serpent," TaMir had said once, "you must remember that they are angriest when they are afraid. The more they bluster, curse, and threaten you, the more fearful they are."

A sound like bones breaking pierced the room. The false wall collapsed in a choking swirl of dust as part of Black's glistening fat stomach heaped into the room. But Black did not seem to notice. She was still straining to push forward around the pillar. "Kill you I will!"

JaRed fled.

Just as he shot into the mouth of the tunnel, the pillar snapped with a sound like thunder. Black's enormous face shot forward and her jaws opened.

The escape tunnel disappeared. The chamber of Wroth vanished. A great wall of rock slammed down into the earth, sealing the tunnel in a dead end as complete as any devised by mouse or prairie dog in the history of Tira-Nor.

JaRed stood suddenly, stunningly, alone. Black was gone. The Chamber of Wroth was gone. Both of them miraculously replaced by a solid wall of blank rock a whisker's distance from his trembling nose.

He stared at the new rock wall, his heart pounding, a cold sweat pouring down his face. His breath came in great heaving gasps.

He stepped back, slumped against the far wall of the tunnel, and slid slowly to the floor.

What he needed now was a long drink of cool water and his very own sleeping chamber.

In a moment he would get up and begin the long walk home.

After his legs stopped shaking.

Chapter Five

Serpent Killer

JaRed awoke to the sound of GrouSer's voice.
"What have you done, you rapscallion? Eh?
What mischief have you worked to shake old
GrouSer's bones?"

JaRed blinked and held up a paw against the light
of the glowstone GrouSer was shoving in his face. "No
mischief."

"What, then? An earthquake? A comet? A herd of
bison dancing a jig over GrouSer's head?"

Two sentries from the kingsguard appeared, wearing stern expressions. JaRed spilled his story slowly, but the sentries clearly didn't believe a word of it.

"A snake?" said the older one, glancing at the wall of rock that had once been a chamber opening.

"I don't smell anything," said the other. "More likely you destroyed the chamber yourself and invented the snake to get out of it."

"But I didn't!" JaRed protested, noticing that the presence he had felt earlier was now gone. "There *was* a snake. I didn't have any choice!"

"Either way," the older sentry said, "the king will want to see you."

♦ ♦ ♦

King SoSheth flew into a sputtering rage when the sentries brought him news of the escape tunnel's collapse. The stress of the rat sightings—coupled with the effects of the drought—had taken a toll on his already depleted patience. Now he was awake again in the middle of the night, jarred into reality from a shallow sleep that had been miserable to begin with.

"It's not enough I must have nightmares," the king bellowed. "I cannot even have them in peace!" He paced in front of the royal dais, his voice rising with his temper. "And now I learn one of the most ancient of Tira-Nor's defenses has been destroyed by a *kit*!" He stopped in front of JaRed, who stared at the floor.

"Well, mouse? What do you have to say for yourself?"

JaRed drew a deep breath. "I dreamed of a snake …"

"Oh. So it was a dream," muttered one of the guards.

Trembling, JaRed told his story for the second time. As he spoke, the royal advisers arrived, including the powerful and suspicious YuLooq.

When JaRed came to the part about waking up and sensing the presence of ElShua, he heard someone say, "The insolent pup," as though JaRed were making it all up.

YuLooq snorted. TaMir raised one eyebrow.

"So I kept going past the chamber of Wroth and found the—well, the snake ..."

"No!" YuLooq interrupted. "How did it get past the switchback? Past the double-turns? Past the fool's errand?"

JaRed stared from face to face. None of them believed him. A few looked as if they expected the king to order his execution. "I don't know," he managed at last. "Perhaps it dug its way. Perhaps Lord Wroth led *it* as ElShua led *me*."

"Lord Wroth!" YuLooq spat, his voice thick with contempt. "Don't give us such nonsense."

JaRed's face burned. "Perhaps ElShua led the snake there for a purpose. Perhaps the tunnel was *meant* to be closed."

"Quiet," the king snarled. He glared at JaRed for a long moment. Then, with terrible calmness, he said, "You have destroyed one of our most ancient defenses, JaRed."

The fact that the king used his name sent a shiver of fear down JaRed's spine.

"Did I not say," TaMir said, "that you should not trust the tunnel?"

The king turned. "What are you talking about?"

TaMir hunched forward slowly, his great white bulk ominous. "Perhaps it was not the boy who closed the tunnel after all. Perhaps ElShua has made your decision for you, Majesty."

"I did not *want* my decision made for me."

"Even if it was the wrong decision?" TaMir asked.

"Are you suggesting this mouse may be telling the truth?"

TaMir sniffed. "There is one way to find out." He looked at the guards. "Did either of you cheese-for-brains bother to send a patrol round to the tunnel's other end to see if evidence of a snake could be found?"

◆ ◆ ◆

As they waited for the patrol to return, JaRed's Father and Mother arrived. Horrid came in just behind them. He leered when he saw JaRed restrained between two of the kingsguard.

Father sidled up to JaRed, muttering something about youthful indiscretions. Up close he asked, "What have you done, JaRed?"

"Yes," Horrid asked. "What have you done?"

Father spun and clapped Horrid across the ear. "For once in your life, HaRed, hold your silly tongue!"

Horrid's face turned crimson.

"I've done nothing wrong," JaRed said.

Father sighed and looked away. Was he concerned about his son's safety? Or merely worried about news of "Runt's Folly" spreading through the city?

Horrid leaned in close. "Maybe," he whispered, "I won't have to tell the king about your treason after all. Maybe he'll see for himself what a fraud you are."

King SoSheth paced the dais, balling one fist into an open palm. "If there really was a snake, how did it get in? What does this say about our other defenses? If the double-backs can be easily breached, are they useful against rats? Or was the snake in league with them? No, No. That's too much for anyone to believe."

Too much for anyone to believe? JaRed thought. *What does the king believe in?*

JaRed imagined himself in the Dark Forest. The cool black shadows, the trees spreading their green canopy overhead, the chirping of crickets. Countless places to hide. Black caverns and sunless hollows and fallen trees. And no one to know that JaRed son of ReDemec even existed. He could really live there, not just exist. He could be free.

There would be water too. The forest was dotted with hidden pools, all green with algae and rippling under the dance of mosquitoes and water-skimmers. If you went far enough into the trees you'd eventually find a stream that poured into a long glassy pond; both stream and pond were unfouled by sulfur and went down the throat as cool as winter rain. That's what the storytellers said anyway. No one JaRed knew had gone far enough into the Dark Forest to see these things for themselves, for not even the kingsguard went more than a half day's march into the trees. But the stories of the Ancients were clear.

The royal prosecutor, a tall, thin mouse with narrow eyes and a neck like a bent twig, said, "Captain Blang's scouts tell me the rats are led by an enormous rat as quick as a ferret and with the teeth of a fox. Fearless. They say it killed a cat."

King SoSheth inhaled slowly, then turned back to his pacing. "Rumors. Nothing more. They're just rats. Slow, lumbering, stupid rats."

◆ ◆ ◆

Just before dawn a young patrol officer knelt in the royal chamber. The king and the prosecutor gathered around to hear his report.

"The scent of snake is very strong around the opening, Majesty. I went in and followed the smell." The officer spoke slowly, and the others exchanged respectful glances. It would have taken profound courage for even a member of the kingsguard to follow a snake into a hole. Only TaMir gazed at JaRed without expression.

"The scent followed the double-turn, then came back. At the extreme length something horrible blocked the passage. A serpent's tail, Highness. Black and very long." The officer glanced at JaRed. "It is not moving."

Silence filled the room.

After a long time SoSheth said to TaMir, "Without the tunnel we shall have to prepare for a siege."

TaMir bowed. "Your Majesty knew all along it would come to this."

"Yes, I knew." SoSheth turned to Captain Blang, his face resolved. "Tomorrow, you will have your engineers close the last of the great holes and redouble your efforts to stock the supply rooms. Narrow all exits with caked mud. Construct new traps, double-backs, and hidden chambers. Activate the reserve militia and begin formal training of all eligible mice. In short, prepare Tira-Nor for battle. I want the city ready for a fight, if fight we must."

"Yes, my lord." Captain Blang bowed.

At last the king turned to JaRed. "It seems we owe you our thanks, mouse. For many lives would have been lost without your courage. What was it they called you?"

JaRed cocked his head, perplexed. Just a little while ago the king had called him by his given name. And now the king couldn't remember it? JaRed remembered what LaRish had said about the king being unpredictable, and he shoved the thought aside. "They call me Runt, Majesty."

"Runt? I see. Perhaps we should call you Serpent-Killer instead? Or Tunnel-Breaker."

JaRed was not sure whether the king sounded angry or amused.

"In any event you have the royal gratitude. I think, unless your father objects, I shall take you into my service. Would you like that, mouse?"

"I would be honored."

"And you?" the king asked ReDemec.

JaRed's father stuck out his chest. "With great pride."

"Very well. Tomorrow seek out — where is LaRish?"

"You threw him out of the palace last week," Captain Blang said.

"Well, never mind that. JaRed, find General LaRish and tell him he is to instruct you along with my son, JoHanan. Tell him he is to prepare you to serve in the kingsguard."

"Yes, Your Majesty. Thank you, Your Majesty."

"Oh, don't thank me. I am likely to need you before you are ready. A war is coming. And it smells of rats."

♦ ♦ ♦

In ElShua's garden a new world bloomed. It had grown much in the past few months. So much that its hole, which had grown with it, now spread like a small pond in the center of the field. The surface of the hole shimmered with starlight.

Then, great sorrow! The stars blinked. The world shivered as though under a tremendous weight.

At the far end of the garden ElShua's shoulders slumped, and a look of deep anguish came over him. "Owl," he called. "Come quickly!"

The Owl came.

"Your first burden." ElShua pointed into the hole. "Go quickly and find a mouse. And understand from now on you will have no rest, for your burdens will be many."

Down the Owl flew, and was swallowed by the now black pool.

He found the soul of the mouse in a dark cavern near the sea, next to its body.

There, too, he found Wroth, as he knew he would. The Owl could see him even if the rats could not.

Wroth laughed. "So? Where is ElShua?"

The Owl did not answer. He only stared at the trembling spirit of the mouse and understood Wroth had been tormenting it.

"Too busy to come himself? Sent an owl to do a

god's job?" Wroth laughed again. "I told you so You'll regret this, I said. Over and over. And still I say it. You'll regret this more than you know. Every time I say it, it means another one of these creatures — these *nothings* — will die. And while I am here killing, you will be going back and forth. Bouncing between here and there like a rubber ball. Between death and life. Regret and hopelessness."

Still the Owl did not answer. It seemed to the Owl he had never understood anything before this moment. Even now he understood so little. Yet here was a mouse, loosed from its moorings. How it trembled!

Gently the Owl spread his wings and took the mouse spirit in one talon while Wroth mocked.

On that day the Owl swore that never again would Wroth be permitted to attend the separation of a soul. Never again would the newly dead suffer the torture of the rat as they waited for safe passage to ElShua's side.

On that day the Owl made a promise to Earth. And to himself. He would come quickly when a body expired. Always quickly. He would swoop from the sky with the wind under his wings and carry the sorrows of a wasted world to redemption. So no poor soul would be left alone, even for a moment, with a suddenly visible Wroth.

Never again would the Great Owl come late to the dying.

Early, perhaps. But never late.

◆ ◆ ◆

HaRed left the palace when he could stand the ingra-
tiating blather no longer. On his way out, he leaned
close to JaRed and whispered in his ear, "Imagine that.
Runt. A soldier."

Then he stomped past the palace guards and into
the dingy corridors of the Commons before making
quickly for his hiding place.

The alcove stood in darkness above a little-used
corridor in the perimeter tunnel south of the ReDemec
home. The alcove held the wooden mechanism of the
Wind Gate wall-stone.

He stopped when he came to the familiar dip in the
tunnel floor. He reached up high on the right-hand side
for the earthen ledge, cool and damp to his touch. He
leaped up into the alcove and lay with his back against
one wall.

He placed one hind paw against the smooth wooden
lever and thought about JaRed's promotion into the
kingsguard. *Ridiculous! Was all of Tira-Nor mad?*

It would serve them right if rats destroyed the
whole city.

He stared into the darkness in the general direction of the lever. A nudge was all it would take. Then
what noise! The wall stone slamming down. The earth
shaking with the impact. The guards at the Wind Gate
falling over themselves in fear. It would be nothing to
evade the sentries afterward. There would be no one to
point a blaming finger at HaRed, son of ReDemec. He
could flee to the Dark Forest and watch as Tira-Nor fell
to the rats.

Such power in one paw! The power to frighten soldiers, enrage a king, close a tunnel for weeks or months or even years. He closed his eyes in the darkness.

Only I would know!

Now *that* was something worth thinking on. For what else did HaRed son of ReDemec know that he could reveal—or keep hidden—at his own pleasure?

Chapter Six

The House of Man

The Corn Field here there be snakes

Tall Grass

Dry Gully

Tira-Nor

Round Top

The Dark Forest

KNOWN WORLD

Winding Cliffs

To The Abandoned Quarry

In the House of Man

I n JaRed's dream, LaRish poked a stubby, gnarled nose into his sleeping chamber and spoke in a far-off voice. "You wish to sleep all the day?"

JaRed rubbed his eyes. So strange, LaRish being here. LaRish of the quick reflexes and even quicker wit.

"You are used to sleeping in, perhaps? But I cannot work miracles. If you would train with the kingsguard, you must get up."

What was LaRish doing here in JaRed's home,

talking about the kingsguard? JaRed yawned and stretched.

"You will perhaps want something to eat?" LaRish asked. "I will just tell Prince JoHanan the newest member of the kingsguard is tired and hungry."

Still JaRed did not move. His mind had frozen solid, like a lump of ice. His body felt as though he were floating between two worlds, somewhere beyond the reach of responsibilities and appointments and orders shouted by grumpy forage masters.

"Why the king should want you, I do not know. But I am a soldier. I follow orders. When the king says, 'Go.' I go. And when he tells me to train a great nuisance of a mouse into the kingsguard, I say, 'Okay.' All of the kingsguard are nuisances. But I must have cooperation."

LaRish disappeared for a moment, and JaRed saw through the portal, behind him in the family chambers, Mother standing speechless, her eyebrows raised.

She clutched both paws over her bosom. "JaRed," she called. "What's wrong?"

Then LaRish sneered again, "What don't you understand, *leetle* mouse?"

JaRed cocked his head and blinked.

This gesture proved too much for LaRish. "I am telling you to get up! Move that *leetle* bumpkin out of the hole and come out into this big great room so I can cuff your *leetle* ears! "

King SoSheth.
The kingsguard.
LaRish.

The ice broke all at once, and JaRed understood: this was no dream.

He scrambled out of the chamber and was relieved to see that only Mother had heard the exchange. The others had apparently left for the day.

"I'm sorry," JaRed said. "I was just so tired—"

LaRish waved the explanation away. "Save the excuses for when you someday get married, if maybe miracles still happen."Before JaRed was fully awake, LaRish was leading him back through the Great Hall and into the expansive, winding corridors of the kingsguard, though he did not stop to explain where the spidery passages led. JaRed hurried to keep up. It occurred to him more than once that this section of Tira-Nor was no longer forbidden to him. He could come and go here as he pleased, a privilege no other member of his family enjoyed. No doubt this irritated his brothers, which was probably why they had not been there to greet the notorious LaRish.

They passed the four sentries posted at the Royal Gate—an entrance JaRed had never before used—and slipped into the warmth of mid-morning.

LaRish led him silently to the training area, a black pool of shade formed by the jaw of a great rock that jutted from the side of a culvert north of Tira-Nor. The rock formed a sort of cave that provided shelter against the openness of the prairie.

"Ho, there, Corporal LaRish," a voice sang from the blackness of the cave. "You are too late for breakfast."

"Ho there yourself," LaRish grumped. "And I am a *generale* this morning. You think because you are a prince I cannot teach you a lesson? I will tell you something. King SoSheth would thank me to teach you some respect."

Prince JoHanan laughed as they entered the darkness. "Who is this, Master Instructor? I do not recognize him."

"Prince JoHanan, meet your new training partner, JaRed son of ReDemec."

The prince dipped his head in a long bow and offered JaRed a smile. "My pleasure."

In person, JoHanan son of SoSheth seemed much smaller than his father. JaRed had never been close enough to the prince to really notice. He had expected SoSheth's offspring to be more imposing. Instead, JoHanan seemed, if not ordinary, then not royal, either. A pair of wide rose-petal ears jutted from his head. A spattering of brown freckles marched along the bridge of his nose to his forehead, and his smile seemed genuine, almost an offer of friendship.

JaRed decided he liked JoHanan son of SoSheth. Someday Prince JoHanan would make a good king.

Or would he?

TaMir's voice came back to him now, whispering through his mind like a great wind, and the shock of it nearly knocked him to the ground: *JaRed, you are the next king of Tira-Nor.*

And Horrid: *We already have a king.*

Again TaMir seemed so close his breath echoed under the rock: *He will hate you for what I have done, but the words are not mine. It is not might that makes right, in spite of what people say. It is right that makes might.*

JaRed had thought TaMir's prophecy referred to Horrid, but now he wasn't sure. The prophecy hadn't been clear. Come to think of it, what prophecy ever was? What if the words meant *JoHanan* would grow to hate him? What if both father and son turned their venom against him?

But I can't be king. I'm not even strong.

JoHanan laughed, and JaRed realized he was staring. "Sorry," he muttered.

JoHanan's laughter continued, clear and unrestrained, and JaRed couldn't imagine such a laugh turning to hatred.

"It's the ears," JoHanan said. "LaRish says if I would just grow tail feathers I'd be able to fly."

"Your father," LaRish said, "took him into service last night."

"I didn't know."

LaRish shrugged. "The king was going to have him *keeled*, but at the last moment, he changed his mind and decided death is too good for him. He say, What is a more terrible punishment? And all the wise men in court, they say, Make him spend every day with LaRish and JoHanan. So here he is."

"Ah," JoHanan said. "You're the one who killed the snake."

"ElShua killed the snake," JaRed said.

"Are we going to get started?" LaRish asked. "Or stand here blabbing all day? JoHanan! Take your stance as point mouse for a three-unit."

To JaRed's astonishment, Prince JoHanan winked at him.

◆ ◆ ◆

They trained all that day, and the next, and the next.

JoHanan expressed surprised at JaRed's reluctance to oil his fur. The other members of the kingsguard thought oil a necessity. It made them slippery, difficult to grab and pin. But JaRed found he couldn't keep it off his palms, which made grasping anything difficult. Worse, the oil acted like a layer of fat; it made him unbearably hot.

LaRish only shrugged as though it weren't all that important. "He is small, Prince. Maybe it is better for him with no oil. Sometimes the instinct is good, yes?"

And that was the end of it.

Summer drew to a close. The stalks of corn in the fields far to the west bent over in death and turned slowly from yellow to black. The endless shafts of tall grass that carpeted the prairie now stood dormant, as brittle as the wings of a moth. Even the Earth seemed little more than a shriveled and rotting husk. Its skin, now hard as bone, lay split into a craquelure pattern of dusty runnels.

Meanwhile, Captain Blang inspired, cajoled, and threatened the mice of Tira-Nor to incredible feats of service. The mice of the Commons were thirsty and exhausted, but they dug, scraped, foraged, hauled, shaped, planned. They formed new booby traps, narrowed the gates, and closed old passages. They plotted and planned and schemed. They stocked the storerooms with more and more food, though most of it hardly looked edible.

JaRed slept in his own private chambers in a section of the palace reserved for the kingsguard. *Like something from a dream,* he thought. His muscles ached, and he slept soundly, though never long, and he gained a new respect for both JoHanan and LaRish. LaRish carried himself with the speed of a cat and the cunning of a hawk.

As he trained, JaRed discovered inner reserves of strength he didn't know he possessed. His family would barely have recognized him, but of course there was no time for visiting relatives.

One night LaRish ordered JaRed and JoHanan to meet after curfew at the training area, and JaRed found himself stalking through sagging tallgrass beyond the mound of the Common Gate. Overhead, a hooked moon washed the field in a blue haze the color of thinned milk.

After curfew, LaRish had said. Which was illegal, and meant sneaking or lying or conniving to get past the guards at one of the gates.

JaRed dealt with this obstacle easily enough, though his solution was perhaps not the sort of clever trickery LaRish expected. JaRed simply took the long way round. Back into the bowels of Tira-Nor. Back to his old stomping grounds, the passages and tunnels of the poor, the place that still felt like home to him. He belonged in the Commons if he belonged anywhere.

Not long ago he had thought the mice of the Commons had rejected him, but now he knew it wasn't rejection as much as containment. He was small; therefore, he would do small things.

But wasn't that the truth? Had he ever really expected to shake the world? To make a difference in the universe? To do great deeds and live important adventures? His only really important adventure had terrified him ... and made the king angry.

Face it, he told himself, *you are what you are. A simple mouse, nothing more.*

When he found old GrouSer on duty at the Tower Gate, he told him the truth. LaRish was running him through some kind of a test on kingsguard business. GrouSer let him through with barely a twitch.

Smiling, JaRed supposed that after being vindicated in the killing of the snake he could tell GrouSer just about anything and be believed.

"You're late," LaRish spat when JaRed arrived. JoHanan yawned groggily in the corner.

"A pass would have saved some time."

"You would I should make it easy for you?"

"Yes, please," JaRed said. All these tests. All these exercises and long days and training rituals. At times LaRish could be irritating.

"Come. Time to go."

They stalked out into the terrible openness and headed west.

Out of sight of Tira-Nor's sloping field, they stopped beneath an old hedge apple tree at the edge of the cornfield that marked the western boundary.

"We must be careful, now," LaRish said. "Their sentries may be sleeping, but I think not."

JoHanan rubbed his paws together. "What's the mission?"

"We are looking," LaRish said.

"For what?"

LaRish twitched his nose. "Rats."

"A spy mission?" JoHanan asked.

"A scouting mission."

"Good," JoHanan replied. "If other mice can be sent on dangerous missions, so can I."

LaRish scowled. "The first test of a good king is what he will surrender for his people. So. What will you surrender, prince big shot? Eh? What do you have that is so much more important than this *leetle* mouse?"

Prince JoHanan blinked. A moment passed before he answered. "Nothing."

"Well, that is what you ought to say," LaRish said. "But still it is wrong. You do have one thing more than JaRed. You have a crown waiting for you. Don't forget that."

"So what are we to do now?" JaRed asked.

"Now we earn the food the king gives us and find out what you are made of. It must be enough, for we cannot help you. Are you ready?"

JaRed glanced at JoHanan and nodded.

"How many weapons have you?"

"Three," JaRed said. "Tooth, claw, tail. The tooth is most natural, but the claw is surprise, and the tail is balance."

"Strike the throat of a rat and he will bleed like any mouse," LaRish said. "Rats are slow and stupid, but don't underestimate them, for they can *keel* more easily than you. But you have other weapons. Behind your nose, yes?"

JaRed stared.

"Your eyes, *leetle* one. Your eyes are not just to look. They are to *see*. Understand? Many mice and many rats look. Not many really see."

They crept forward silently. North along the line that divided corn field from prairie.

It took careful navigation through the concealing tallgrass before they found a clear view of the subdivision. They stood on a little rise looking west through parted blades.

Men called the massive structures *houses*, though how they could live in such grotesque monstrosities JaRed could not imagine. The trees in the subdivision had been leveled months ago. Here and there a yard of cultivated sod broke the tedium of dirt, concrete, and gravel. A few of the houses were evidently completed, ready to be lived in. But up close, on the eastern edge of the development, there were still empty lots for sale.

In the corner lot nearest them, a house under construction stood outlined by the light of the moon. Though fully framed, two of its walls were unsided, and its studs threw long, shadowy ribs across the new driveway.

LaRish poked JaRed in the side with one paw and pointed. "There. Do you see them in the burn pile?"

JaRed looked, seeing nothing but a stack of discarded lumber and assorted construction materials. "I don't see anything."

"I do," JoHanan said. "There's a great fat one at the far end."

Now JaRed saw it. A rat, motionless, standing sentry in the shadows of the pile. As he looked, he saw movement farther back. "More than one," he said.

LaRish nodded. "Many more. Probably two hundred in that pile. They are gathering here to attack Tira-Nor."

"With only two hundred rats?" JaRed asked.

LaRish shook his head. "Two hundred *in each pile*. Did I not say to use your eyes, *leetle* one?"

JaRed began to understand. For every house there would be a trash pile, and in every trash pile two hundred rats were hunkered down, waiting for the command to attack and drive the mice of Tira-Nor from their home. "But that means—LaRish, how are they doing it?"

"It takes time to move such a large army. But rats are not patient. Many have been here for weeks. Their leader must be powerful indeed to keep them together so long."

JoHanan whistled softly. "If the stories are true—"

"Do not trust stories. Rats are moved by only two things: hatred and fear. When they obey, it is because they are afraid or because they hate. They will attack us for both reasons. They fear this master of theirs, and they hate us."

"But why?" JoHanan asked. "What have we done to them?"

"Done?" LaRish spat. "You needn't have done anything to be hated. Some creatures hate because they don't know anything else."

"What do you want me to do?" JaRed asked.

"Count them," LaRish said. "As close as you can. We must know how many they are."

JaRed nodded.

"I brought you because you are small, JaRed. Because you can make yourself invisible. This is better than big muscles or sharp teeth. Go and see without being seen. Then come back here and tell me. Be brave, JaRed, but not foolish, yes? "

JoHanan nudged LaRish with one paw. "I'm going with him, right?"

LaRish shook his head. "You make too much noise when you walk, Prince. You sound like the ox."

"I do not!" JoHanan protested.

"Besides, you must be able to count higher than ten."

"When I am king, LaRish, I will demote you to private."

JaRed pushed through the screen of grass and padded down the rise to the boundary of the closest lot. The moon cast a long shadow on the back of the house, and JaRed stayed in darkness all the way to the concrete wall of the foundation. He crept forward to the corner and peered around it to the burn pile.

The rat sentry stood fully awake and was walking toward him. Moonlight glimmered in the rat's beady eyes. It cocked its head to one side, sniffing.

Klogg. Klogg of the thunderous legs and dull brain. Muttering to himself as he paced.

"One two, one two," Klogg burbled. "And not a whisker of food to chew." He turned, sniffed, and ambled the other direction. "Hunger and rot is all we've got. When GoRec's around that's quite a lot. One two, one two."

JaRed waited, willing himself to perfect stillness. He would blend in. He would disappear. Sweat beaded on his forehead. His nose twitched, and he wanted badly to scratch a place behind his ear. But when at last he looked again, Klogg had shuffled behind the burn pile, with only his shadow visible on the far side.

JaRed glanced back to where LaRish and JoHanan lay concealed, but he could not see them. He shrugged inwardly and nosed around the corner. He could think of no other way in.

He darted through the full force of the moonlight, praying Klogg would not round the corner too soon. If Klogg sounded the alarm he would have no chance.

He kept close to the foundation, speeding the length of the garage, and rounded the far corner without even looking back. He fled over the cool, moist concrete of the freshly poured driveway and retreated into the doorless mouth of the garage.

Had Klogg seen him?

No sound came from the burn pile except the distant murmur of Klogg's complaining, and no other sentries were visible.

Through the open garage doorway he could make out two other burn piles. Their irregular heaps were twisted and made grisly by the light of a street lamp that funneled its yellow cone over them. Discarded spears of splintery gray lumber poked outward like weathered bones. The other burn piles were hidden by the bulk of the other houses, or were shrouded in black up and down the street.

Time to move on. It might be safe here, but he could learn nothing by staring from the inside of a garage. He would have to cross the street. Either in darkness — but in full view of Klogg on the northeast side of the house — or under the light of the street lamp, where he could be seen by anyone who happened to be watching.

He padded toward the street, concealing himself in the darkness of the concrete steps of the front porch. The yard was all dirt and weeds and wild tufts of dead grass, unlike that of some of the other houses, which had been carpeted in sod.

He moved forward through the dirt, from shadow

to shadow, his paws as light on the earth as the evening breeze.

At the curb he stopped under the saw-toothed leaves of a dandelion, his head outlined by the lamp-shadow of its white and fuzzy crown.

The black ribbon of street lay before him on the other side of a concrete gutter drain. The street was hard as rock and bald as the smooth pate of Round Top.

For a while he simply stared at the two burn piles. He saw no movement, no sentries. He saw no flicking, hairless tails. Nothing moved in either pile.

But he could not be sure. Not until he got close enough to see, to hear, to smell. Up close he would be able to see the rat droppings, hear the tell-tale snoring, smell the odor of their unwashed bodies. Or he would be able to see that the piles were empty, that the rats had not come in so great a force as LaRish feared.

But he would have to get close enough to see which it was.

He would have to cross the street under the light of the lamp.

He searched the sky for winged enemies. Rats were not the only hunters he feared. But he saw only the spangled blackness. Light from the street lamp ruined his night vision, and his eyes were not so good as the owl's. One never saw the white death before it came. Or if you did, you were already too late to do anything about it.

He took a deep breath ... and ran.

He jumped, tore through blinding yellow light, reached the far side, and left the pavement with a leap that gave him wings. He buried himself in the shadow of a paper bag and lay very still, listening.

He had not been seen.

He peered around the corner of the bag, still in shadow, and stared at the closest burn pile. He sniffed, but could smell nothing. It didn't look as though it were infested with rats.

He moved closer, across a gravel-strewn lawn, to where an empty paint bucket lay on its side. He was almost on top of the pile now. If anything were awake and watching from inside, it could scarcely miss him.

He moved closer.

His nose nearly touched a piece of torn fiberboard siding. A yellow fungus grew on the end of it, and on the whole it smelled of sawdust. Dark, irregular holes into which he could not see glared back at him, but no rats.

JaRed skirted around the north side of it, aware that Klogg, if he were paying attention, might conceivably see his movements from across the street. He swept through moonlight to the next pile, but it too was unoccupied.

He felt lighter. Perhaps the rat army was not so terrible as the other scouts had imagined. Perhaps someone had exaggerated. He returned to the first pile and stalked back to the curb.

Now to make it back to the far side of the street and go home.

He was halfway across before he saw the eyes looking at him from the open grate of the sewer drain.

Eyes like empty wells. Black and cold and hard, like windows into a bottomless pit. Filled with *nothing*.

JaRed didn't stop. He didn't slow down, nor did he change his course.

He sprang for the weeds and flashed like a bolt of

gray lightning back toward the hill where LaRish and JoHanan waited.

Those eyes! They were rat eyes. But how could they be? They were too far apart, too cunning, too large.

Unless they belonged to the rat leader, the one they called Master.

JaRed stopped halfway across the lawn, a blind panic rising in his chest.

Looking down and mumbling to himself, Klogg rounded the corner of the burn pile that lay between the two closest houses and was making his way toward him.

JaRed had nowhere to go. He couldn't make it past Klogg to safety. It was too great a distance. Klogg needed only to bar the way with his great bulk and sound the alarm. In seconds the place would be crawling with rats from the pile.

JaRed bolted to the open concrete of the driveway, more than fifty paces from the garage, as the moon turned its blue-white treason against him.

He turned—slowly it seemed to him—and saw rats leaping into view, gushing in a disordered line from the drain onto the street. They popped into existence like something from one of the old stories: the birth of evil, which knew no childhood but came full grown into the world.

The rats seemed confused and angry. Their posture and their expressions told JaRed they had been only recently awakened.

Klogg apparently noticed neither JaRed nor the other rats. His voice fell in muffled bursts as his pacing brought him closer to the space between the houses.

"One two, one two. Is that his nose or a stinking shoe? One two ..."

If he were coming from the other direction, JaRed thought, *I'd try to run past him.* But there wasn't room.

Klogg looked up. His eyes fixed on JaRed for a moment.

Behind JaRed, several rats squealed, but a voice like thunder quieted them with a word: "Silence!"

Klogg looked beyond JaRed to the street, and his eyes widened.

JaRed fled into the darkness of the garage. He leapt over the threshold of the doorway inside and raced over the plywood subfloor. He took the stairs in an effortless blur. Up and up. There was nowhere else.

He found himself in a hallway on the third floor and decided in a flash to hide in the room at the eastern end. Two of its walls were sided, so it lay mostly in shadow. He huddled in the corner, his nostrils assailed by the strange odors of cut wood, paint, glue, and other things he could not distinguish. Here and there a loose piece of discarded lumber lay forgotten in the darkness. His body shook.

I should not have come here. I should have risked running past Klogg and the burn pile.

But there had been no time to think. Besides, it was too late now.

He was trapped. They were coming for him. A whole army of rats. Wroth's army.

He lay very still and listened.

No wonder the burn piles had been empty. They weren't hiding in the burn piles. They were in the rain sewers!

And why not? It hadn't rained for weeks. There might be thousands of them in there by now. All they would need on the surface would be a few sentries. One burn pile as a lookout post. And when the time was right ...

The moon shone dully, its snowy light painting the floor in stripes through the long studs of the unsided walls. The night air seemed cooler here. The sweat of exertion and fear brought goose bumps beneath JaRed's fur.

Voices stirred in the space between the houses. JaRed heard nothing from inside the house. Indeed, the house still seemed empty.

Perhaps the rats had not seen him go into the garage. He hardly dared to hope.

A voice like thunder boomed from the ground below one skeletal wall. "Which way did he go?"

"Which he do you mean, your greatness?" Klogg's voice rose from the emptiness below, higher and lighter now, airy with fear.

JaRed crept silently across the plywood floor and peered down into the empty space between the two houses. Far below, the burn pile spat out sentries who formed a semicircle behind Klogg and glared at him.

The height from which JaRed looked down staggered him. The world tipped, yawned, drained away.

He thought of the Great Owl and his daily dive for prey. What must the Owl see when he leaned into the earth, pitting his great silky wings against the weight of the world?

JaRed felt a rush of wind, as though he were actually falling, pitching forward into the looming nothingness.

Below him, rats from the sewer flowed around the burn pile, washed against the foundations of both houses, and settled into a frothing mass. They were the biggest rats JaRed had ever seen, and they moved in unison, like some kid of special guard.

Yes. A rat kingsguard. To guard the rat master.

LaRish's voice echoed in his memory. *How many are there?*

His task was to count them. But how could he? There must be hundreds. And surely these were not all. They would not rouse an army just to hunt one mouse.

We must know how many there are. Think, *leetle* one!

He bent forward and counted. Ten. Twenty. Fifty in that knot by the wall, with maybe five knots between the houses. He added the numbers in his brain. Two hundred fifty huge rats. And more swarming over the driveway. And probably more still were emerging from the sewer.

Which meant there must be thousands under the earth. Thousands who hated Tira-Nor and had sworn themselves to its destruction.

In his mind JaRed saw them coming, scrambling through the familiar tunnels of Tira-Nor like water breaking from a dam. An ocean of hatred pouring through the fur-cozy tunnels of his city, biting, squealing, killing. Propelled by a demonic fury even the kingsguard could not resist. Tira-Nor would not survive. It couldn't. Hopelessness swept over him. Pushed him down. Drove him chest first into the wood so hard he felt his breath leaving him.

The creaking of lumber in the night breeze came like laughter from the throat of Lord Wroth.

JaRed shuddered.

Then, as JaRed looked, *it* stepped out of shadow and into the full light of the moon.

The hugest rat JaRed had ever seen. Bigger than he thought possible. Large as a full-grown rabbit. Its movements were as effortless as a weasel's. It didn't shamble when it walked. It *flowed.*

GoRec. King of rats.

The monster growled, and Klogg stumbled backward, apologizing all over himself before finally cowering in submission.

JaRed felt a brief stab of pity for him.

GoRec said nothing at first, just raised up on his haunches until he towered over the shivering Klogg.

"You," GoRec bellowed. "You allowed one of their spies to get away!"

Klogg hunkered down, as though by seeming smaller he could avoid notice. "Puh—puh—please."

GoRec's body seemed to waver in the moonlight, swaying once, twice, three times above Klogg.

Then GoRec struck.

The movement was so fast JaRed barely saw it. One moment GoRec was standing on his hind paws, the next moment his teeth were in Klogg's throat and he was shaking the smaller rat like a dog killing a snake.

JaRed couldn't bear to watch the killing. *No,* he thought. *I won't look.* He backed up, his throat closing into a knot.

But then he couldn't resist. He crept forward and peered over the edge again, telling himself that seeing could not be worse than imagining.

He was wrong.

JaRed turned his head as the rats cheered. What sort of monster was this? What kind of creature took pleasure from another's suffering?

He did not move for several moments, but simply stared at the sky, the unblinking stars, the black emptiness. In the distance long wisps of fog drifted over the trees of the Dark Forest.

Without warning JaRed felt the presence again, its stillness and majesty so tangible his head felt heavy under the weight of it. He was not alone.

In an instant he stopped worrying about himself, about how he was going to get past the new sentries at the burn pile. He thought only of two equally necessary things: *escaping* the presence of ElShua, and *keeping* the presence of Elshua.

"My Lord," he whispered.

He heard no answer, but the presence grew stronger. JaRed ducked his head, tried to press his body into the plywood flooring. But then, without willing it, he stepped forward. His left forepaw grasped the head of a rusting ten-penny nail, cool to the touch.

His paw shook. Sweat stood in beads on his forehead. He must, somehow, pick up the nail. But why? What madness was this?

A voice as clear and distant as the moon whispered, "JaRed." So soft, yet it splashed into the room like a waterfall.

"Lord." JaRed had never felt so helpless, as though his body and soul were being sucked into a whirlwind, as though the air itself were being peeled back like skin off an onion.

"Don't be afraid," the voice said. "Take the iron stick. Be a fang for my venom."

Then it was gone.

◆ ◆ ◆

As the years passed, the Owl's burden of soul-bearing grew wearisome indeed. One day, as he carried a tiny shrew in his beak, his temper snapped like a dry twig.

He landed in the garden behind ElShua and spat out the shrew in the sunlit field.

The shrew's body had withered in sickness. Its life had ebbed away so slowly, and in such loneliness, that at last not even the insects, not even the worms, not even the earth had noticed its passing. And if the earth had not noticed, then why must the Owl? Did ElShua even care? Then why should the Owl? What was one shrew to the Great Owl?

The shrew's eyes opened slowly and drew joy from the air of the garden. But the Owl took no satisfaction from the soul's rebirth.

"I'm finished," spat the Owl at ElShua's mountainous back. "I can't take it anymore. Banish me if you must, but I'll never carry another soul unless you tell me why. Well? Tell me, Lord. Why don't you bring them here yourself? See them in their misery with your own eyes? Well? Who am I that I should stand in your place?" The Owl cast his fury at ElShua's great shoulders, the shoulders that held up the sky. "I'm too small for this task. Too small, I tell you. It's not my fault! And I can't take it anymore!"

ElShua turned to face him, and suddenly the Owl could not speak.

Great rolling tears slid down ElShua's face.

The Owl saw in those tortured eyes a misery larger than the universe. He saw the death of the shrew in those eyes. And not just the shrew's, but every death. Every disappointment. Every stab of treachery and rejection and regret. As though the pain were burned forever in long, jagged scars across his mind.

"Friend Owl," ElShua whispered at last, "listen carefully. And let my words give you strength and courage. Or if not strength and courage, then fear. For I will not tell you when this shall be, nor what form I will take when it happens. But one day you will come into my wounded world for a dying soul, and that soul shall be *mine*."

"But—" said the Owl.

"You will not recognize me then," ElShua continued. "You will see only a sparrow, or a fox ... or a forgotten shrew. You will not know me until you have brought me here."

"But," the Owl said again.

"Therefore," said Elshua. "you must carry each soul as though you carry me. For one day you will. Do you understand?"

ElShua held out his hand and the shrew leapt into his palm. And oh, what a leap the shrew made!

"Friend Owl," ElShua said. "All this time you have been faithful. You have brought many souls to my side. You have seen them remade. You have seen their tears wiped away, their sorrows transformed into laughter. And yet you still carry their grief in your heart. Did you not know your burdens must be carried one at a time? Did you not know you must leave them with me?"

And ElShua reached out with his empty hand and broke the Owl's neck.

The Owl gave a startled cry, his eyes widening in agony. But as suddenly as it had struck, the pain vanished. For ElShua had already healed the wound with his fingertips.

The mice of Tira-Nor say ElShua recreated the Owl that day. He made the Owl's head to spin. He made the Owl's eyes wide. Since then the Great Owl is always straining to see in every direction, looking for the dead.

They say, too, on that day the Great Owl stopped shifting blame, for it was not just his neck and eyes that were remade.

ElShua gave him a new heart.

Which is why the Great Owl asks every passing cloud where his next burden lies.

Which creature shivers at the point of death? Name a name, clouds! Name a name, trees! Tell me quickly!

"Who?" the Great Owl demands.

◆ ◆ ◆

JaRed waited in the house until GoRec and his warriors returned to the sewers and the rat sentries went back to the burn pile.

Oddly enough, the one sentry who remained on guard did not seem any more attentive than Klogg had been. But then, JaRed supposed there was nothing more to fear from GoRec tonight.

It seemed the point of Klogg's murder hadn't been to punish him for his offense, but for the sheer sake of punishment. To kill just for the pleasure of it.

When the sentry appeared to be sleeping, JaRed slipped out the garage door and ran back to the hill, wondering if LaRish and JoHanan would still be there.

As he passed the burn pile he saw Klogg's body lying in a broken heap across a crushed cardboard pizza box. He could not help thinking that even Klogg did not deserve such a death.

LaRish and JoHanan met him halfway up the hill.

"I'm hungry," JaRed said, feeling he could eat barrels of food.

"You waited long, *leetle* one. This is good. It shows patience — something *you* could learn, Prince."

JoHanan whistled. "Did you *see* that monster?"

"Yes," JaRed said.

"And did you see his weakness?" LaRish asked.

JaRed frowned. "I saw his speed."

"He was quick, yes." LaRish spat. "Almost as quick as me, and that is saying something. But I mean something else. This rat, he has a weakness. What are you carrying?"

JaRed held up the nail. "A gift." The nail felt heavy and awkward in his grip.

"Who is it for?" JoHanan asked.

"Me."

LaRish stared at him for a moment, one eyebrow raised. "I think maybe you are going soft in the head, *leetle* mouse."

Chapter Seven

YuLooq

HaRed son of ReDemec the Red muttered a long and heartfelt curse, full of hatred, directed more or less at the center of the universe.

Gray clouds marched across the sunless sky, empty promises of rain that made HaRed's throat burn with thirst. Even nature taunted him now, reminded him again of his own, not to mention Tira-Nor's, desperate need for water.

HaRed labored outside with the rest of the commoners, foraging for anything that might be stored and consumed later. King SoSheth was preparing for siege, and all foraging parties had been ordered to double duty. They had been working almost constantly for over a week without a decent rest.

All of which was Runt's fault! Runt was the reason they all suffered, for he had destroyed Tira-Nor's only escape route. Runt had trapped them in a massive grave with no better plan than double duty for the scavenging parties. While he avoided scavenging by posing as one of the kingsguard.

What a wretched plan! Wait for the rats to come. Wait to die of thirst or be torn apart by the claws of rats. Wait to die, because a thoughtless piece of garbage had destroyed the city's back door.

HaRed clenched his teeth. Why had the king promoted the little scum? He looked around at the other scavengers. They were all tired and thirsty, he knew. They had all been forced into long days of labor with little to eat and little rest. Now even the elderly and infirm were working outside as scavengers.

I've had enough of that pompous brother of mine and his irritating self-righteousness. Surely by now the king would believe what HaRed had to say. Surely by now the king had seen through Runt's posturing, his false humility, his incompetence. The little flea-biter wasn't capable of ruling a chamber of mouse-kits, let alone a great city like Tira-Nor!

Time to see King SoSheth.

HaRed found, after an interminable search, a small cache of dirty sunflower seeds, which he pressed into the pouch of one cheek. Not much, but enough to justify a trip into the storage chambers off the Great Hall.

It would have been faster to go straight to the Royal Gate, but the kingsguard would never have let him through. What he needed now was a bit of trickery, something he—like every mouse of greatness—had always possessed in large quantities.

He found the blood-red berry he had buried in an empty walnut shell in preparation for this moment. He cast a wary glance around him, but no one paid him any attention. He put the berry in his mouth, and though it had dried out in the last two weeks, what moisture was left exploded in his mouth. He barely kept himself from swallowing it in his thirst. Instead he spat the juice onto his left paw, then swallowed the skin of the berry. He licked at his new "wound," pleased with the effect.

It looks bad, but not awful. He headed for the Common Gate, limping.

The gate sentries barely noticed HaRed's limp and waved him through when he showed them the sunflower seeds.

Inside, the smell of fear filled the city. The barracks around the Great Hall now billeted hundreds of conscripted militia from all areas of the city. Volunteers trained for battle in the tunnels and at defensive positions. New traps were being dug, new switchbacks and double-turns and wall stones installed. Passages were being narrowed to create more easily defensible posts. Some were being closed altogether, caked with mud to dry into a kind of cement that would be difficult for rats to burrow through. Most of the passages leading from the Commons to the barracks of the kingsguard were being sealed, as well as the tunnels between the

Commons and the Families. The Commons, which lay closest to the surface, was apparently expected to fall first.

In a store room now bulging with seeds, cones, nuts, dried berries, and other supplies, he deposited the sunflower seeds from his cheek, then turned and shuffled back to the main corridor. There he turned right instead of left and hobbled to a side passage leading down.

He knew the way. A side passage to the Great Families, a section of Tira-Nor no Commoner would be allowed into without good reason.

The sentry at this guard chamber looked him over carefully. "Are you all right?"

"Fine," HaRed said, grimacing. "Just ... just a thorn, that's all. Hurts, but I'll be okay."

"It looks bad. You ought to have it looked at."

HaRed let a hint of pain twist the corner of his mouth. "You think so?"

"No sense letting it get infected. We're going to need able bodies soon."

"I suppose you're right. But I have an appointment with Master YuLooq. And I mustn't keep him waiting."

The sentry waved aside his objection. "You're in luck. There's a doctor two chambers down from YuLooq. You can ask him to look at it on your way. Tell him OoRay sent you."

A less intelligent mouse might have taken the direct route to the king through the guard chambers of the kingsguard. After all, many of the passages would be completely sealed soon. But HaRed knew such an approach would mean an intolerable delay waiting for an audience that may never happen. HaRed preferred subtlety.

After proceeding a safe distance, he stopped in the darkness and licked the berry juice from his paw. It wouldn't do to be found wandering in the chambers of the Great Families with a blood-stained paw. Someone might mistake him for a common soldier.

◆ ◆ ◆

The attack came late in the afternoon.

JaRed stood sentry atop the dome of Round Top, but he did not see the first rats until they were almost upon the skirmishers.

His position left him exposed to the sky, and the temptation was to look *up* when his duty lay in looking *out*. True, there was a tree to huddle against. But mice do not like heights, and they feel vulnerable when surrounded by too much open air. Captain Blang believed such vulnerability helped his sentries to stay alert. JaRed often found himself looking over one shoulder, half expecting to meet the talons of a hawk.

He focused his gaze on the western horizon, the direction from which any attack would surely come. Occasionally he glanced north or south, but his attention was always drawn back to the houses of men.

Beyond the houses lay the unknown lands, about which almost nothing was known. Even in the oldest stories and songs the realms beyond were rarely mentioned. Other than TyMin, who had come to Tira-Nor from the southwest, there remained in the collective histories only hints of the forgotten things from the far world.

He stared west at the peaks of new wood gables that pierced the dusty rim of the sky. He brushed one paw against the shock of white fur at his forehead.

The earth shuddered.

Fear rose in his chest, and all at once he seemed to be falling, the same sensation that had terrified him the night GoRec slaughter Klogg and left his body on the burn pile like a broken toy.

A scene unfolded in JaRed's mind as the sky pressed down on him, suffocating in its enormity. The air grew heavy. He felt he was drifting away and down, sinking into the dirt and clay and gravel, into the bedrock and the hot molten heart of the world. The waking vision grew stronger as he plummeted.

Away to the north and west lay a vast prairie dotted by woodlands, rivers, and lakes. A sea of homes — the houses of men — flowed in a relentless current of wood and plaster and paint toward Tira-Nor. Beneath the current ran an intricate web of sewers, and in the sewers gathered a horde of rats.

But only for a moment.

Then the vision shifted. From sky to grass he fell, tumbling, and at the same time he seemed to be rising through water, as if to catch his breath after long submersion.

He passed through a vacant lot that lay like a missing tooth between two ancient brick buildings, and stood under a sign that towered above him on iron legs bleeding rust at their bolted seams. Red letters blistered and fell away from the white surface, leaving the faded outlines of words:

The Springer Meat Processing Plant
WELCOME

The vision at last slowed, drawing JaRed closer to the earth beneath the sign. For a moment he circled the ground like water going through a drain.

Overgrown with weeds and withered bluegrass, the earth here was littered with rotting plywood and bald tires. Empty liquor bottles glittered in the afternoon sunlight. A doorless refrigerator leaned awkwardly to one side, its stomach stained yellow by some long-forgotten accident. Wild tulips grew here and there, as though in defiance of the ugliness around them.

At the epicenter of the vision all motion stopped, and JaRed saw a long, lean rat between the concrete feet of the sign. The rat was thin, a death mask of starvation stretching over its face. Long crescent ribs showed through a thin pelt, revealing sick legs and a neck no wider than a twig.

The rat's eyes shifted nervously, and JaRed felt a sudden stab of compassion.

"Who are you?" JaRed asked.

The rat looked up, whiskers twitching on its gaunt face, its eyes black and empty and afraid. It did not reply.

On Round Top, JaRed backed into the prickly bark of the tree, blinking away the vision. To the south, the brown-leafed oaks of the Dark Forest marched into the distance beyond the White River.

JaRed did not know what to make of the things he had seen. Had he been dreaming? Or was it something else?

He saw one of the foragers. Two dozen or so still scampered through the field, the last of the day, scurrying to get something — anything — to fulfill their quota and allow them entry back into the safety of a dark sleeping chamber inside Tira-Nor.

JaRed caught the flick of a tail in the distance.

Odd. The tail was too far west. Someone must have strayed dangerously far from his assigned position.

Except ...

The tail was too long to be that of a mouse.

JaRed took a deep breath and waited. No sense sounding a false alarm. The scavengers were tired and did not need to waste their energy running from a sentry's mistake.

Then came another flick, another tail, and more movement from the west. Too far west. The dry, yellow, tall grass, bent over in death but still carpeting the field, seemed to move, as though the earth were caught in a slow shudder.

JaRed sat up, straining to see.

The earth indeed was moving, a slow current of motion too distant to be grasped but too large to be denied. It was as though a wave of dirt were washing slowly toward him from the far side of the field, on top of which the ground cover heaved and sagged like flotsam on the surface of the sea.

"JoHanan," JaRed said. Then, louder, "JoHanan!"

The prince's voice came from below. "Yes?"

"Something is happening."

JoHanan's nose appeared in the rocks below. "What sort of something?"

"I don't know. I can't describe it. Tell LaRish to sound the alarm."

"Why? What do you see?"

JaRed struggled for words. He struggled for air. A cold shiver of fear crept upward along his spine. "I see ... a wave," JaRed said softly.

JoHanan sniffed the air below an exposed root at the ledge. "A wave?" He frowned. "What kind of wave?"

"I can't describe it. I don't know what it is."

"Are you sure it's not just the wind?"

"It's not the wind," JaRed shouted in frustration. The wind did not blow in a single line. And if what he saw was wind, the whole field of tall grass would be bent over.

"All right, all right. No need to snap at me. But I can't tell LaRish to sound the alarm because you saw *something*."

JaRed took a deep breath. fighting back his old familiar insecurities. JoHanan was just like the others. Just like his brothers. Just like Horrid. They never believed him. Simply because he was small.

The wave continued rolling, slow and steady like the tide. It crossed a quarter of the distance of the field on the far side of Dry Gully. In moments it would break against the scavengers. And then what?

JaRed felt words come out calmly from a place inside himself he did not know existed. "Tell LaRish I'm not looking. I am *seeing*." His voice sounded like someone else's, as though he were a bystander listening in. "And what I see is the earth about to swallow up Tira-Nor."

JoHanan's mouth opened and closed soundlessly. Then he leapt down the closest side of Dry Gully, crossed to the far side, and disappeared in a yellow quilt of stalks.

Somewhere between the wave and the scavengers, JaRed saw a long, fat tail flick in a bare patch of earth. Skirmishers. Scouts. Raiders at the head of an army so massive that when it moved, the whole world shuddered.

Lord Wroth had unleashed his fury.

The rats had come.

◆ ◆ ◆

HaRed stopped at the entry to the great house, which was expansively lit by glowstones. Green light spilled from the opening into the passageway in an obvious boast of wealth.

Not that anyone in Tira-Nor was ignorant of the owner's prosperity. YuLooq's opulence rivaled — perhaps even exceeded — that of King SoSheth, though of course his power lay not in birthright but in politics. YuLooq was a mouse of prestige, one of the advisors to the king, and a wealthy merchant who understood how to turn ordinary vice into profit. True, he had gotten old and fat, but what was power for if not to make you comfortable? Though he would not have admitted it, HaRed envied the old creature.

A servant came quickly, sniffing the air as though testing it for a sign of HaRed's good breeding. "May I help you?"

HaRed stroked his whiskers with one paw. "I wish to see Master YuLooq on a matter of urgent business. Kindly let him know HaRed son of ReDemec the Red has arrived."

The servant's brows narrowed. He paused a

moment, then seemed to make up his mind. "Very well. Wait here." He scurried off.

HaRed shifted his weight from side to side, leaned his head against the wall, and eventually sat in the entry and stared at the ceiling.

At last the servant returned with a look of satisfaction. Self-importance, arrogance, and stupidity all mixed together on his face. Apparently the direct method had not worked, though in truth HaRed hadn't expected it to.

"Master YuLooq is unavailable," the servant droned. "Perhaps sometime next week, if you would be so good as to send a messenger in advance, a private audience could be—"

HaRed stood, shaking his head. "There isn't time, fool!" He stepped into the green bath of the foyer and leaned in close to the servant's twitching face. "I don't believe you really told Master YuLooq what I said." He spoke softly, knowing a whisper would be more menacing than a shout. "But because I am a nice chap who is easily misunderstood, I'm going to give you another chance."

The servant glanced to either side.

HaRed knew what he was thinking. *Where are the other servants?* But HaRed also knew there *were* other servants, and he would need more than an intimidating manner to gain an audience with YuLooq.

"Now," HaRed continued, "you will go back to Master YuLooq and you will introduce me. You will use my name and my father's name. And you will use my brother's name, Runt. And this is what you will say ..."

A moment later the servant whirled into one of the many openings that led deeper into the house. HaRed wondered if he had overplayed his hand. What if the servant were merely cowering in some dark antechamber, too frightened to do anything?

At last YuLooq came, accompanied by two tough-looking bodyguards who did not seem like the sort to be easily intimidated. YuLooq scowled. "What do you want?"

HaRed bowed. "Master YuLooq. Thank you for allowing your humble servant a small morsel of your time. You will not be disappointed."

YuLooq sat on fat haunches. "I am already disappointed," he said in a low sandpaper voice. "I was dining. You interrupted me."

"Please accept my apologies. But this matter is urgent. You may remember that a few weeks ago my brother, JaRed, also known as Runt, was commended by the king for a supposed act of service that left the escape tunnel of Tira-Nor permanently and irreparably destroyed."

"What of it?"

"The king seemed most displeased."

"Perhaps. But wasn't this brother of yours promoted to the kingsguard?"

"Indeed he was. Yet I suspect his promotion was born of necessity rather than good will."

YuLooq squinted, then cocked his head to one side. His lips and lower jaw moved as though chewing a bit of grain he had found between his yellowing teeth. "What do you want?"

HaRed decided to be blunt. "What would I get for

bringing to the attention of the king certain information about a traitor bent on usurping the crown?"

YuLooq whispered to the bodyguards. They glanced at JaRed and left. The old mouse waddled nearer, his movements ominous. "That is a curious question, for the one who asks it may be worse than the one he pretends to reveal. Intrigue is no game. Your reward might be a slow, painful death at the hands of the royal prosecutor. Are you sure you know what you are doing?"

HaRed cleared his throat. "Quite sure."

"Of course, you *might* receive the royal gratitude." YuLooq smiled briefly. "If your information proves correct."

HaRed gave another bow. "Not that I expect any reward, of course. My only desire is for the safety of my king. However, I am sure you understand the necessities and practicalities of life. To be frank, my talents are wasted. I have labored among commoners all my life. Not to complain, of course. ElShua knows we need commoners. But it seems to me the commoners who labor in the scavenging parties ought to be, well, *common*, if you take my meaning. Surely it would benefit both His Majesty and the blessed city of Tira-Nor were I to work where my services can be most profitably used."

YuLooq's eyes narrowed. "I believe something could be arranged. Quarters in the Lesser Families perhaps. Along with a monthly stipend. And a Title. It would of course depend upon the information."

"I am quite certain the king would be interested to learn that the treason I speak of has originated very close to his own heart."

YuLooq squinted. "How close?"

"One might say it is so close *even a seer* would not reveal it to him."'

YuLooq squatted in the center of the room. His gaze flicked upward, as though he were tasting some delicious morsel of food. "That is quite an interesting thing to say."

HaRed bowed more deeply.

"And how did you come to know of this treason?"

HaRed licked his lips. "I was there when it was born."

Chapter Eight

The labels visible on the map: The House of Men, Tall Grass, Tira-Nor, The Corn Field here there be snakes, Dry Gully, Round Top, The Dark Forest, Winding Cliffs, The Abandoned Quarry, KNOWN WORLD

Round Top

The alarm saved most of the scavengers' lives. A few paused, as though not believing the attack could really have come. The rest fled immediately into Dry Gully. Though already exhausted when they heard the signal, they seemed to find new strength.

JaRed watched them scramble down the wall of loose dirt and limestone, then up the opposite bank, panic written on their faces. Their fear was fueled by the unknown, making it hotter and more insistent.

They fled from something they had seen in their imagination a thousand times, but never in real life. This was just as well, for if they *had* seen, they may not have found the strength to run.

JaRed waited for LaRish and JoHanan—the rest of his three-unit—to come from the grass on the far side. Kingsguard units did not leave one another behind in battle.

Before LaRish and JoHanan had emerged from the tall grass of the opposite slope, JaRed saw to the north the nose of a black-and-brown rat sniffing the open air. The rat paused, then saw the gray flash of a fleeing mouse and charged after it down the embankment. A score of other rats appeared near the same spot, just to the north.

JoHanan shot from the grass on the opposite bank, followed closely by LaRish. They scrambled up the side of Dry Gully just below Round Top. Behind them, six rats gave chase.

JaRed peered down at JoHanan from the temporary safety of his stone perch. JoHanan jerked his head toward Tira-Nor, meaning JaRed should go back alone.

JaRed didn't move. It was too late for any of them to make it back to the city unscathed. The first skirmishing rats to the north had already cut off their line of retreat.

"LaRish," he shouted. "JoHanan! Turn back. Turn south."

JoHanan apparently did not hear. He kept streaking along the narrow, grassy path that lay between the high upper bank of Dry Gully and the sloping limestone wall of Round Top. He was coming closer to JaRed's perch ... and closer to more rats.

LaRish swung himself up onto the path behind JoHanan from the gully, then looked back. Behind him, rats poured over the opposite bank like flood water breaking over a dam. He looked up at JaRed as JaRed continued to voice his warning.

"Go back," LaRish shouted up at him. "That is an order." Then he flew after JoHanan.

The battle of Dry Gully ended in less time than it takes to read about it. Like all battles, it consisted mostly of confusion, fear, pain, death, and surprise. The stories of fierce bravery and unabashed cowardice would be remembered later, long after the fighting ceased. In the suddenness of the moment words like *courage* and *fear* didn't exist. There was only the feeling of one's breath catching in the throat as time slowed to a crawl.

JaRed watched the brown-and-black rat slink toward the mouth of the grassy pathway to the north of Round Top, its fur oily and flecked with foam. There was little JaRed could do. The path down Round Top lay on the eastern side of the hill. To get to JoHanan and LaRish he would have to go the long way around. The western slope dropped off in a sheer cliff taller than a full-grown man. JaRed could *look* down, but he could not *get* down. Not without serious risk of injury. And JoHanan did not know what lay just ahead of him as he retreated.

The two enemies collided with rib-crushing impact. The rat, who was moving more slowly, took the worst of it. He fell backward into the gully, a look of terror contorting his face as he clawed at the air. He landed like a bag of flour on a rock sun-bleached to the color of an old bone.

JoHanan almost fell with him. Indeed, he would have fallen had LaRish not been there to grab him by the fur of his neck and pull him back to safety.

Below them, the injured rat cursed and threatened them from the gully floor.

The other rats closed in from both sides, two from the north end of the ledge and dozens from the south.

LaRish and JoHanan stood back-to-back on the grassy ledge, trapped between the converging rats.

LaRish brushed aside his whiskers with one paw. "So," he said to the massive black rat edging ever closer to him. "I am to *keel* first a lieutenant, yes? What is wrong with you, lieutenant rat? Why do you come so slowly? Do not tell me you are afraid of a *leetle* mouse?"

The insult worked. The black rat charged.

LaRish waited, his body seeming to melt into the ground. For a split second JaRed thought LaRish had waited too long, the rat had gotten too close, and La-Rish would be pinned beneath the larger body. But LaRish twisted and heaved, leveraging the rat's force in one continual motion that carried the surprised creature over LaRish's back into the yawning space above the gully.

In an instant the other rats closed the distance. They swiped, clawed, and bit, shrieking the fierce and distinctive war cry that sounded to JaRed like the cries of a thousand tormented souls.

JoHanan dispatched one of the rats with a bite to its throat, but another rat blocked their retreat. A great monster with mottled fur and a whiskerless nose pinned JoHanan on his back and poised to rake the prince's belly with his hind claws.

JaRed leapt. He had no plan; he knew only that he could not let his friend be ripped open. He hit the rat's head with his shoulder a split second before he struck the ground. The rat gave a grunt of pain and was thrown halfway off the ledge.

A shaft of fire stabbed JaRed's chest. Pain exploded in a white-hot ball around his heart, and his jaw stretched open. His lungs quivered weakly but would not open to draw air. He lay on his back, his legs twitching as though he were reaching out for his own departing soul.

JoHanan rolled away, kicked out with his hind leg at the mottled rat's face, missed, and tried to stand. The rat pulled itself back up onto the ledge and grabbed one of JoHanan's legs.

JaRed heard cursing to his left. He turned his head and saw rats piling up single file behind LaRish, calling on Lord Wroth to smite all mice with lingering diseases, lightning, and death.

JaRed's breath returned in a rush. He sucked in great gulps of air and turned onto one side. The fire in his chest subsided, but a long line of pain ran down his spine. He shoved the pain aside and drew himself up on wobbly legs. Yes, he could stand, but could he run? Well, he would have to.

The mottled rat pulled himself back onto the ledge and blocked the path. His sides heaved as he panted for air.

Unfortunately, the same thing that prevented the rats from converging in force on the three mice—the narrowness of the ledge—also worked to their advantage. There was not enough room for the mice to use their natural quickness in such a close fight.

What the mice did have was a strategy of cooperation, something the rats had never fully developed. The rats of the west rarely cooperated for any reason other than fear. They knew nothing of loyalty or covering another rat's back. Many of them had watched their companions torn to shreds by GoRec and laughed about it.

But now only one rat lay between the three mice and the Shade Gate. JoHanan and the rat seemed to understood this almost simultaneously. A look of grim determination spread across the rat's face. It hunched down, gathering itself for a tremendous blow.

JaRed did not wait. He charged, darting dangerously close to the ledge, and bit the rat on the ankle.

The rat gave a startled cry just as JoHanan delivered a resounding kick to the point of the rat's nose.

The rat howled miserably and fell backward against the cliff wall, clutching his nose with one paw and his wounded ankle with the other.

JaRed pushed JoHanan forward, past the rat and toward safety. "LaRish," he cried. "Come now!"

LaRish, who seemed to be enjoying himself, knocked a fourth rat over the ledge, then followed JaRed and the prince up the slope toward the Shade Gate. The rats followed, but were not fast enough to catch them.

"I thought you didn't like running from rats," JoHanan said as they ran.

"I am a *generale*," LaRish shouted. "I subscribe to the ancient wisdom of Frevoirzheis!"

"What's that?" JoHanan asked.

"Fight like a man," LaRish said, "but run if you can."

◆ ◆ ◆

GoRec's skirmishing force came across Dry Gully to the north and headed for the city in a ragged line. On the lower slopes of the field, kingsguard mice rose up from their hiding places in the grass and brought the line of rats to an abrupt halt. The West, Open, and Shade Gates would be kept open as long as possible before the wallstones were tripped.

It was no secret that members of the kingsguard were often arrogant. Sometimes they were condescending, too, for the king regularly pampered them with meals from his table. Commoners envied the kingsguard for their position of prestige and relative luxury. Members of the kingsguard did not have to labor in the fields.

But the kingsguard were also exceedingly brave. When the terrified scavengers began to return to Tira-Nor, screaming, "Rats! Rats!" the kingsguard mice leapt into action. Each warrior scrabbled for his place at the head of the line, hoping to be among the first to come to the defense of the defenseless. Each knew that later they would face the king and, worse, LaRish, and none wanted to be last out of the barracks.

Small battles erupted near West Gate and North Gate, which had to be closed after an orderly retreat. Mice, fighting in the open in their disciplined three-units, inflicted great damage to the first of the rats, who seemed surprised at the intensity and effectiveness of Tira-Nor's initial resistance.

Kingsguard mice wounded two dozen rat skirmishers and suffered only two seriously injured mice.

Not a great strategic victory, but an important one for morale. When Captain Blang saw he had established a temporary but firm perimeter for any remaining scavengers who might be slow in returning, he turned to the last limping and terrified mouse to hobble through the line to safety.

"Where is LaRish?" he asked. "Where is Prince JoHanan?"

The tiny mouse shrugged. "Behind us, my lord."

Captain Blang cursed the rats under his breath and looked around.

An unplanned truce fell across the battlefield as the rats retreated toward the tall grass to regroup. A silent, heavy peace settled on the bleeding combatants. Mouse warriors sucked in great gulps of air, glaring ferociously at the ever-increasing horde of rats. Opposite them, new rat fighters arrived on fresh legs, bearing unbloodied hides and expressions of hunger.

"Lieutenant KoVeek," Blang snapped.

At once a young officer appeared by his side. "Captain?"

"I need five volunteers in the next thirty seconds. Let it be known that any who come with me will probably not come back alive. When I am gone, you will command the retreat into Tira-Nor."

"Where are you going, Captain?"

"To find Prince JoHanan and General LaRish."

KoVeek took a deep breath. "I wish to come with you, Captain."

Captain Blang shook his head. "I need you here, Lieutenant. Now, get me those volunteers."

KoVeek started to argue, but stopped when he saw Blang's expression. "Yes, Captain."

Then, as KoVeek turned to go, Captain Blang touched his shoulder. "Wait a moment. Look to the Shade Gate!"

Coming from behind the rats, LaRish, JoHanan, and Runt were almost on top of the skirmishers, attacking from the rear.

Close to the thinly defended Shade Gate, the rat line turned, swelled, and buckled as if struck by a giant fist. Three rats went down in a tumble of flying fur and twisting claws. Screams, shouts, and curses drifted across the prairie.

Several rats, recovering more quickly than the others, tried to jump onto the twisting mass of tails and teeth. But only one landed any kind of blow. Mouse warriors from the kingsguard recognized what was happening and rushed forward to form a protective line.

JoHanan and LaRish broke free, leapt the few lengths to the safety of their peers' protection, then glanced back.

But JaRed son of ReDemec had disappeared.

◆ ◆ ◆

JaRed saw the clawed fist of an enormous rat, its fur caked with sewage, a second before it delivered a stinging blow across his cheek. He twisted to his right, and the rat's second blow landed with the force of a hammer on his shoulder.

JaRed gave a cry of pain as the rat's claws sank into his flesh. Blood pulsed onto his fur in a long, jagged line.

The rat hissed into JaRed's face a foul stream of breath as rotten as an old cabbage. "That," he snarled, "is for Lord Wroth."

Thanks to LaRish's training, JaRed attacked without thinking. He kicked up with his hind legs, arcing his back for strength, and felt the claws of his rear feet bite into the rat's belly.

The rat shrieked and leaned back to avoid JaRed's kicks ... just as JoHanan hurled himself into the rat's vulnerable ribs.

The rat's mouth opened in surprise at this new pain.

"*That*," JoHanan spat, "is for having bad breath."

The kingsguard closed around JaRed as more rats spilled from the grass to the north, coming like a wave, stretching, it seemed, to forever and beyond.

LaRish yanked JaRed to all fours. "You can run, yes?"

JaRed nodded, the pain in his shoulder white-hot as nausea roiled in his stomach. His heart pounded like a sledge-hammer against his chest. The world swam. It seemed he had been fighting and running and fighting and running for days.

He looked again to the north and west, but it took a moment for him to see the truth of what was happening. The sight sent a shiver of renewed terror down his spine.

A flood of rats crashed from the cover of the leaning tall grass and swept toward them in a horrible, swollen mass of black and brown. This was the earthen wave he had seen from the dome of Round Top. This was the main body of GoRec's army, come at last to lay siege to the city of promise.

But the sea of rats was not the worst of what he saw.

GoRec, king of the rats, came with them, surrounded by his own sort of kingsguard, the Ur'Lugh. They were perhaps two hundred of the fiercest rats JaRed had ever seen. They moved in disciplined ranks, like seasoned warriors, not topsy-turvy as rats usually do. They were all huge, all well-oiled. As they approached, JaRed saw that each of the Ur'Lugh warriors had smeared half of his face with reddish-black war paint.

No, JaRed realized, not paint. Blood.

A collective hush settled on the mice.

"I told you to retreat," LaRish huffed, his breath coming in gasping heaves as he spoke in JaRed's ear. "Is that what you call … obeying an order? I have half a mind … to claw you myself. But I am too tired. And besides … I have not thanked you yet."

JoHanan nodded toward the advancing army. "We haven't much time."

LaRish grinned. "Let's go, then. Take JaRed inside."

"What about you?" JoHanan asked.

LaRish scowled. "I am a *generale*. I will come last. My *honair* is at stake."

JaRed didn't argue. Helped by JoHanan, with the kingsguard covering their retreat, they reached the Shade Gate and plunged inside.

After they were all safely encompassed by the comforting blackness of the tunnel, JaRed looked around. Female mice tended the wounded, licked their wounds. Now that the immediate danger was past, some of the warriors openly shook with fatigue and fear, all sense of dignity ignored.

But JaRed knew: LaRish hadn't followed them through the Shade Gate into the tunnel. He had never intended to.

LaRish was still outside.

Chapter Nine

LaRish

From his position at the head of a small line of defenders, Captain Blang stared in quiet disbelief at what he saw unfolding to the south. Numbness crept over his mind, settling around him like a warm blanket. When he spoke, the words seemed to come from someone else.

He ordered his mice to retreat into a tightly controlled circle, though the nearest rats had broken off their attack and seemed content, for the moment, to await orders. Now the rat battalions stood in a ragged line less than three meters away.

Blang's mice obeyed with admirable precision, closing their line into a tightly ordered island of safety around the narrow hole of the one gate that would remain open.

To the south, the last of LaRish's exposed kings-guard mice slipped inside the Shade Gate, but LaRish did not enter. Instead, he wheeled around and moved toward the knotted mass of the Ur'Lugh on the open plain.

Captain Blang drew a sharp breath. "What is he doing?" he snarled to no one in particular. "Doesn't the fool know we need him?"

By tradition, the last defending warrior outside a besieged a city was considered a messenger. This was a matter of functionality more than courtesy. Someone had to take the terms of the attacking army inside to the king. Until this moment, Captain Blang had expected to be the one who would execute this unfortunate duty.

LaRish clearly had other plans.

◆ ◆ ◆

The rats could have fallen on LaRish from all sides and ripped him to pieces, but something held them back. Perhaps it was his self-assurance. Perhaps it was his irritating and belligerent smile. Perhaps it was the blood smeared on his fur, none of which seemed to be his. Whatever the reason, the great sea of rats gave way before LaRish as though he carried a terrible disease. A poet might have called that disease *courage*, but the rats were in no danger of catching it.

The rats parted around him like the waters of the

White River in the ancient story. The Ur'Lugh warriors sneered, then glanced back at GoRec for instructions.

"Let him through," GoRec said. His voice sounded like gravel.

The Ur'Lugh did as they were told, and LaRish slipped through their lines to stand before GoRec.

"You have come for terms," GoRec said. "You shall have them. I give the mice of Tira-Nor one hour to leave the city."

"I have not come to hear your pathetic demands," LaRish said, "but to see if you are as good a fighter as the rumors say. I am told you do very well against females and kits."

GoRec scowled. "For that, you will die slowly."

"Well, I have lived long enough. And you seem to have lived a bit too long. You have attacked innocent mice without warning. You have *keeled* without provocation. You have surrounded Tira-Nor to take what you can never have: *honair*. I would give you a worse insult than this, but I cannot think of one. You, sir, are a rat!"

The Ur'Lugh formed a large circle around the two, a sort of combat ring for the duel. They laughed as though they had no doubt what the outcome would be.

LaRish glanced to his right, toward the sloping mound of the West Gate, where Captain Blang stood his defiant watch.

GoRec hissed, rose, began to sway.

"Pay attention, Captain Blang," LaRish said in a voice audible only to himself. "Or this will be for nothing."

◆ ◆ ◆

HaRed tried not to reveal his surprise when he saw the wealth of King SoSheth's palace for the first time. He was good at hiding his thoughts and emotions, but even so, he drew a sharp breath when—after what seemed an eternity of waiting in an adjacent guard chamber—he at last stepped into the private chambers of the king.

Blue and green glowstones washed the room in a soft cascade of light, giving the chamber an iridescent, liquid appearance, like moonlit water. The walls and floor were carpeted in matted down, soft as the fur of a kitten, and seemed to radiate warmth. At the far end of the room, the king reclined with YuLooq as a serving maiden fed them raisins.

The guard who had led HaRed into the room bowed low, his nose touching the floor. "Your Majesty. HaRed son of ReDemec the Red."

The king barely glanced at him. "Who are you and what do you want?"

Before HaRed could answer, YuLooq swallowed a bit of raisin and raised a finger. "Forgive me, Majesty, but ..." He turned to HaRed. "We met previously, did we not?"

They had spoken less than an hour ago in the guard chamber, where YuLooq had advised him to *"be patient and play along, and look for opportunity as the conversation progresses."* But HaRed understood that in the game of politics the most important rule was to never say what one meant. "I am at your service, my

lord. My sincere apologies for this unfortunate interruption, Your Majesty."

"Apology accepted. Now, what do you want?"

"I am here, Highness, because I have information
that may be of interest to you."

King SoSheth licked one paw. "Information? No.
What I am interested in is raisins. Servant! Must I grow
them myself? Thorns and thistles!"

The serving maid appeared with two more raisins
and handed them over, bowing profusely.

King SoSheth bit the end off of his and chewed
thoughtfully. "Excellent. I must see that the last of
these are moved to my private quarters." He motioned
to HaRed with his empty left paw. "Well, mouse? Get
on with it."

"King SoSheth," HaRed said, "you have taken into
your service a certain mouse by the name of JaRed."

"Also son of ReDemec," the king said with no hint
of irony.

HaRed cleared his throat. "My brother, in fact."

"Unremarkable."

YuLooq raised one paw. His eyes shone dully in
the light of the glowstones, and for a moment HaRed
saw himself reflected in the blackness of each pupil. "I
believe he's the one who destroyed the escape tunnel,
Majesty."

King SoSheth scowled. "Well, *that* was remarkable.
The little serpent killer. What about him?"

HaRed looked to YuLooq. The old merchant's fat
face smiled, stretching into an expression as cold and
hard as ice.

"Majesty." HaRed's voice seemed to come from

somewhere far away, somewhere dark and lonely and desperate. "My brother JaRed has been anointed king over Tira-Nor."

♦ ♦ ♦

Captain Blang's mind was numb. He could not think. A dreadful sense of inadequacy and fear swept over him.

It couldn't be. And yet it was. The monster of his memory and the rat master GoRec were the same rat!

He knew. He saw. He heard. The memories — the sounds and sights and smells of that night — came flooding back, undimmed by time.

Shush. Be still. Father will protect us ...

Mother hiding him in the secret hollow place where he could peer out and see Father defending them. Father the commoner. Father the fearless. Father, who stood up to two, then four rats, circling among them like a mongoose among serpents. Father biting, wheeling, arcing.

Father bleeding. Father killing.

Until the monster came. The huge rat with the blood-frothed nose, the pink bubbles at his lips, the dark stains on his teeth. The monster rose up like the heavens and struck.

Father falling. Shuddering under the impact as Mother screamed ...

"Captain Blang?"

Lieutenant KoVeek's impatient chirping drew him back to the present.

GoRec, the one who had killed Father and Mother and all the rest, had come at last to Tira-Nor.

"We must get inside. We can do nothing for him now."

Far down the sloping plain to the south, GoRec's Ur'Lugh warriors closed into a tight fist around LaRish and the monster. Even the legendary LaRish would not be able to fight his way out.

"He is a brave mouse, sir, but there is nothing we can do. He is buying us time to secure the city. Let us not waste it."

Without taking his eyes from the circle, Captain Blang said flatly, "No, Lieutenant. We will wait."

"But sir—"

Blang cast a withering glance at the lieutenant, who snapped a stiff salute and shut up.

As Blang turned back, the Ur'Lugh exploded. The great knot of rats that encompassed LaRish swelled and opened as two rats went down, falling on themselves as if struck by some mighty blow.

Indeed, they had been struck. By GoRec. Probably by mistake, though Blang could not tell for sure.

As the fist opened, Blang was able to see. A timeless battle: dwarf against giant, hopelessness fighting fear. A dance of death. A dance of spinning grace and grotesque force and spit and blood and sweat.

The bodies seemed to flow together as they struggled, the two dissimilar creatures meshing into one live, writhing mass of furious will.

Eternity pressed upon him. The moment expanded until nothing but the *now* mattered. Blang felt as though he were going into war himself.

He caught a glimpse of LaRish spinning, whirling, biting. LaRish taking a long, bloody gash along his spine as GoRec's claws swept past him and LaRish slid away. LaRish, as light as the wind, dancing and weaving on paws that seemed tiny by comparison. LaRish striking in his inimitable style, moving in, under, turning lightly.

And yet not so lightly.

LaRish was tired.

Blang could see it, though perhaps the rat could not. But then, Blang was familiar with LaRish's style. And LaRish was not so young as he used to be.

GoRec struck, missed, recovered. He coiled. He sprang. He missed again.

Strike now, Blang thought. For he saw the opening he could not have seen as a child on the day GoRec killed his father. The rat was vulnerable at the throat. When he struck downward his front paws opened, and in that instant there was space for a death blow.

Surely LaRish saw it, too. Three times GoRec had struck in the same fashion. Each time from the left. Each time after swaying. And each time his front paws opened for an instant. Just an instant. But long enough.

LaRish did not take advantage of the opening. Instead, he turned like a leaf tossing in the wind, arcing out of the way, barely a hair's breadth from the point of GoRec's outstretched claws.

The gash on LaRish's back widened as long fingers of blood reached down his ribs. Too much blood. Long stripes that burned black in the trailing sunlight.

The blood loss had taken its toll. LaRish was beyond tired. He was exhausted.

He cannot win.

GoRec rose up as the Ur'Lugh cheered. LaRish spun again, moving in this time, though more slowly. He bit a chunk out of GoRec's thigh, drawing a scream of pain and rage so deep even the Ur'Lugh were silenced by it.

LaRish's sides heaved. He did not back away, and Blang knew LaRish had no more strength left.

Blang heard Mother's scream. Saw the look in Father's eyes as he died: a look of profound helplessness and sorrow, a look of exhaustion, a look of defiance that would burn itself forever into Blang's memory.

Father!

GoRec spat a stream of profanity audible even from where Blang stood. He cursed mice, Tira-Nor, ElShua. His mouth foamed with a pink froth that he wiped away with the back of one paw, rage making his limbs shake.

LaRish drew himself up. He turned toward the deserted mound above the Shade Gate and lifted one paw in a silent salute.

GoRec struck.

◆ ◆ ◆

JaRed shot from the Shade Gate into the sea of rats and raced for the circle of Ur'Lugh warriors. The guards at the narrow mouth of the gate would have tried to stop him had they seen him coming, but his exit was so unexpected they didn't have time to react.

Rats of all shapes and colors surrounded him, though none were so large as those in GoRec's bodyguard. It seemed GoRec had pressed all of the largest rats into the Ur'Lugh.

They let JaRed pass without a word, parting as they had for LaRish. Not all the rats were as ferocious as the skirmishers he had fought earlier. Most of them seemed small by comparison. And ordinary. They smelled like garbage. But they were still rodents, even if their tails were ugly and bald. JaRed imagined most of GoRec's army consisted of simple rats, commoners like himself.

He wondered how many even wanted this war with mice. Perhaps some of them secretly breathed the name of ElShua when they went to sleep, or when they spoke to their children of life and death, justice and mercy.

He stopped at the circle of the shouting Ur'Lugh. Their voices gurgled, a sound like asphyxiation, and it took JaRed a moment before he realized they were giving a kind of cheer. He did not know why. He could not see through the ring of tall rats, and he could not tell what had happened.

When one of them finally noticed him, a grotesque sneer spread across his face. He tapped another rat on the shoulder. When they had parted, JaRed saw LaRish lying like a bundle of rags on the ground, his fur matted and torn.

Bleeding from a dozen minor wounds, GoRec wiped the bloody froth from his mouth with the back of one blood-stained paw. He sneered at JaRed. "Another champion?"

JaRed stepped into the ring, which closed behind him, and padded over to where LaRish lay staring into the sky.

"That's no champion," one of the Ur'Lugh said. "They must have sent him for the body."

"Good," GoRec said. "Take it back into Tira-Nor with my terms for your surrender. Any who surrender before dawn will be spared. All others will die slowly, like this one. This mouse will bleed to death within the hour. And he will suffer much in the meantime. Let this be a lesson to your king."

The Ur'Lugh laughed.

JaRed hovered over LaRish, too numb to think.

"*Leetle* mouse," LaRish whispered, "did you see?"

JaRed shook his head. "Hang on." The rats could have killed him then and he would not have resisted. It seemed the world had already come to an end.

"It is ..." LaRish wheezed, his voice coming in great, heavy gasps as blood rattled in his throat.

"Don't talk," JaRed said. "I'm taking you back into Tira-Nor."

"It ... is ... an ... *honair*."

◆ ◆ ◆

JaRed could not lift LaRish. He hooked his paws under the armpits and dragged the body backward one staggering step at a time. It took a long time to reach the Shade Gate.

Three times Blang sent soldiers to demand permission to help remove the body. And three times the demand had been rebuffed by attacks from the rats.

Clearly the rats were enjoying the situation. They taunted JaRed as he struggled to get the body inside.

They turned the whole thing into a cruel game. No mouse would help him, and no rat would inhibit him.

JaRed felt nothing. The world of rats all but disappeared. He barely heard their mocking laughter. He did not heed their voices, their threats. The universe shrank to a long, narrow tunnel, a path of flattened grass that stretched for what seemed miles between here and the Shade Gate.

LaRish's body grew heavier with each step.

JaRed was tired. His legs were stumps of wood, fixed by fatigue into a cramped mass of knotted muscle. Worse, the oil on LaRish's coat made getting a firm hold nearly impossible. Now JaRed's paws were smeared with a mixture of oil and sweat and blood. With each step, he was forced to shift his weight and readjust his grip.

Reach under LaRish's ribs with the opposite hand. Glance briefly behind him. Grip the lower shoulder. Step backward.

Do it again: Shift and adjust. Look behind. Step.

Shift. Look. Step.

Like some awful, bloody dance. Like the rhythm of life itself.

So much blood. Why should there be so much? Where did it come from? The blood of mice, the blood of rats. Where did it end? Would it end with GoRec's blood? King SoSheth's? JaRed's own? Would it ever end at all?

Blood from the wound in LaRish's back seeped onto JaRed's chest, where it congealed into a warm, sticky mat. The sun fell.

Shift. Look. Step.

Time stood still, and all movement and sound became a blur. The taunts of the rats were like water running in a stream, flowing indistinguishably past, lost in a current that bore away the universe. Everyone and everything slid into the beyond, into darkness, falling endlessly over the edge of reality.

Shift. Look. Step.

In his mind JaRed saw the white sign on its rusting legs. He stood beneath it, looking down at a starving rat with eyes like empty wells.

"Tweener hungry," the rat said. Fur jutted from his body in thick strands, like pieces of string.

"Eat something," JaRed whispered.

The rat closed its eyes. "The Meatsies and the Dumpsters hates Tweener. Cruel they are!" He gave a long, shuddering moan that might have broken Ja-Red's heart had there been anything left to break.

Shift. Look. Step.

"The Meatsies has plenty. The Dumpsters has plenty. Tweener has nothing."

A voice spoke from the stream of time, from the vision, and it sounded like ice breaking to pieces on a swollen river: "They don't understand you, do they?" Full of cold sympathy. Bursting with lifeless generosity.

"No," Tweener said. "Dumpsters and Meatsies the same. No one helps Tweener. Tweener lives alone."

"Ah," said the Voice. "All alone in a terrible world."

"Yes. And hungry. Always hungry, always small. No one ever —"

"Poor Tweener!" the voice cut in. It echoed in Ja-Red's ears like a thunderclap. "Living between two gardens of plenty, yet always without. Do you know why some mice call themselves Meatsies and why others are Dumpsters? It is because they have plenty, Tweener. Plenty! Ah, yes. The Meatsies live in a world of hanging meat, always there for the teeth. The Dumpsters' land is filled with the most lavish excesses of the earth! Over-ripe bananas and half-eaten sandwiches and berries and breads and delights Tweener cannot even imagine. But do the Dumpsters share?"

"No," Tweener said miserably.

"Do the Meatsies?"

"No," Tweener whispered.

Shift. Look. Step.

"But then," said the voice, "that is the way of mice, isn't it?"

Tweener moaned.

"Yes, that is the way of mice." The voice sighed. "Without food, you will never grow. And if you never grow, how can you avenge yourself against the cruelty of mice?"

"You see!" Tweener exclaimed.

"I see. You want to hurt them."

Tweener seemed to think for a moment. His eyes reflected in the light of the dying sun. "Tweener does," he said at last. "Much much much."

"You want to make them pay?"

"Yes!"

"For every cruel joke, every vicious bite, every damnable thing they've done to you?"

"All and more! Ten times more!"

"Ah, Tweener," said the voice. "There is a way. If only I could trust you."

Tweener licked his lips as though he sensed something wonderful about to slip through his grasp. "Trust Tweener! Tell the way to pay back the Meatsies and the Dumpsters!"

Shift. Look. Step.

"Very well," the voice said softly, like a dying breath. "I will make you great and strong and terrible. I will give you an army of rats. And you will fill them with your hatred!"

◆ ◆ ◆

Captain Blang watched JaRed's struggle from his perch outside the West Gate, his teeth clenched, a quiet fury raging in his soul. The runt was so small. It seemed to take forever.

When at last JaRed had hauled LaRish's body inside the Shade Gate, and Blang's most trusted warriors had retreated into the hole behind him, he stood there a moment longer.

The honor of being last meant nothing now. Captain Blang had been at the wrong place at the wrong time. He had not been a part of the fighting today, and the sense of futility that gripped him was almost unbearable.

He dared the rats to attack him. *Let the whole army descend on me here!* He would show them what one mouse could do!

But the line of rats didn't move.

And so, as the sun fell into the black web of the Dark Forest, Blang descended into the despair of the besieged city.

Chapter Ten

The Siege

Despite GoRec's implied threat, the rats did not attack in force the next morning. A few half-hearted skirmishes broke out around the Tower and Seed Gates as GoRec tested Tira-Nor's defenses, but the kingsguard refused to respond to these feints.

Stationed at their emergency posts throughout the city, the militia passed the day telling stories and speculating about the rat army. Females and kits huddled in their private quarters and waited for news.

In the afternoon, gate sentries reported no less than seven hawks circling the skies, drawn by the smorgasbord of rat flesh on the plain. GoRec's army apparently could find no place above ground where they could all hide at once.

"I never thought I'd be grateful for hawks," JoHanan said to JaRed as they sat in the blue-lit antechambers of the palace.

"This war won't be won by hawks," JaRed said.

"Well, it won't be lost by them either. I pray they eat well tonight."

JaRed shrugged. "It won't make any difference. At this rate it would take months to whittle GoRec's army down to a manageable size."

"GoRec," JoHanan said. "How come those hawks never pick *him* for a meal? They couldn't ask for a bigger target."

JaRed knew the answer, but he didn't voice it. *Because Lord Wroth is with him.*

"I suppose they don't want indigestion," JoHanan said.

JaRed sensed JoHanan was trying to ease his pain, but he wasn't in the mood for laughing.

"What do you think he'll do now?" JoHanan asked. "Do you think he'll try a frontal assault?"

"No," Captain Blang said from the entry. "I expect he'll try to starve us out. Or he may try to burrow new holes into the Commons by moonlight. How's the shoulder, JaRed?"

"Fine," JaRed answered, surprised at the coldness that had crept into his voice. The nightmare of dragging LaRish's bleeding body inside the Shade Gate had changed him. He felt as though all emotion, all hope, had drained from his heart.

Captain Blang nodded grimly. "I am told GoRec himself is waiting at the West Gate for a parley. King SoSheth wants you to be there, JoHanan."

The prince rose. "Come with me, JaRed. If you're up to it."

JaRed nodded. "Wouldn't miss it."

◆ ◆ ◆

Outside the Shade Gate, GoRec stood alone, his Ur'Lugh warriors arrayed in a semicircle behind him. King SoSheth, Prince JoHanan, Captain Blang, and JaRed watched from the guard chambers just inside the hole.

Even though the ground on which GoRec stood sloped downward from the gate, he towered above their heads. But JaRed could tell by the way GoRec's eyes moved that he could not see into the darkness of the hole.

King SoSheth edged closer to the shaft of light that speared the tunnel near the opening. "Speak, rat," he commanded, his voice calm and clear, the sound of leadership.

GoRec grinned, revealing long and jagged teeth. "Are you the king of Tira-Nor?" The gravel in his voice rattled under the weight of the words.

"I am. What do you want?"

GoRec's grin twisted his face, as though he were about to scream. "I have come to see the mighty Tira-Nor. My new home. "

SoSheth's face twitched. His eyes narrowed to slits. "You must have taken a wrong turn at the corn field, rat. Your home is the sewer."

GoRec threw back his head and laughed, and inside the tunnel the earth shook. "It is easy to cast insults from the safety of your pretty tunnel, king. But it takes no courage."

King SoSheth edged closer to the hole. "If that's what's bothering you, why not come inside, rat? I will insult you to your ugly face."

GoRec laughed again. "I would, but you have narrowed the hole with caked mud, and as you can see, I will not fit. It appears, oh mighty mouse king, that I am not really welcome inside. I must change that."

Behind him, the Ur'Lugh snickered.

"Must you cower in your tunnel?" GoRec growled, his voice lower, more hostile. "Why not come out and fight me, one on one, as a king should? You can see my guard has drawn back. I promise it will be a fair fight."

"Fair?" JoHanan blurted. "That monster is twice your size, Father! And faster than LaRish."

Captain Blang nosed into the tunnel next to King SoSheth. "Let me have the honor of fighting him, Majesty."

King SoSheth sighed. "Brave Captain Blang. You are too valuable to gamble on something as fragile as honor."

Captain Blang frowned and looked away. "Then let him bluster. An owl will pluck him from the earth before the night has passed. Even a blind owl could not miss something that big."

But no owl came, and the next morning GoRec

stood outside the Shade Gate and issued his challenge to all of Tira-Nor as the kingsguard huddled in their fortified chambers, too humiliated to speak.

"Who will fight me? Is there not even one among you with the courage to die like a warrior?"

But Tira-Nor remained silent.

◆ ◆ ◆

HaRed awoke in darkness. To make movement by the militia easier, SoSheth had ordered all glowstones in the Commons be moved from private chambers and gate defenses into the corridors. The family chambers had been black for three days now.

Morning still stood at a distance. So what was this noise in his ears? He strained at the air. Something almost too faint to be heard, and yet persistent, rattled in his sleeping chamber. His whiskers vibrated with the sound, and instinct screamed warnings that the sound could not be natural.

A scratching noise like claws dragging through sand came from the tunnel outside the ReDemec home.

He licked his lips.

No, not the tunnel. The sound came from behind him, from the earthen wall at his back.

He turned in the cozy sphere of emptiness that was his sleeping chamber and pressed one ear against the stone-smooth dirt of the wall.For a moment he hardly dared to breathe.

Then the noise came again, unmistakably louder.

Scratch. Scritch-scratch-scraaaaatch. Scratch. Scritch-scratch-scraaaaatch.

He huddled there unmoving a moment longer, listening to different spots along the wall. He finally cupped a paw behind his ear to focus the sound.

Scratch. Scritch-scratch-scraaaaatch.

He understood suddenly, and fear gripped him.

He bolted into the entry to the family quarters and froze there a moment, thinking. Should he tell Father? No. He couldn't. Father and KeeRed had drawn evening duty in the militia and weren't home. He thought about waking Mother, but decided against that too. There was nothing for her to do, and she would only worry. And KahEesha was spending the night with a friend in the lower levels of the Lesser Families.

He padded to the hallway and sniffed the air.

West. He must go west.

He ran to the third intersection on the right and dove south along the familiar perimeter tunnel now only barely lit by glowstones every thirty lengths.

The militia expected GoRec to send his main attack into the center of the city, where it could not easily be contained. As a result, the perimeter tunnels were patrolled thinly by older mice who were considered too weak to be of much value in the main battle.

But now a feeling of impending doom twisted in HaRed's gut. What if King SoSheth and the militia commanders were wrong? What if the attack came not in the center, but from the edge?

He stopped and put one ear to the tunnel wall and held his breath. In the near darkness it seemed the whole world had come to a sudden and desperate end.

Scratch. Scritch-Scratch-Scraaaaatch.

HaRed's heart skipped a beat, quivered, then thudded like a stone in his chest.

They were coming. Now. Here.

GoRec's rats were digging a borehole at the perimeter, and once it opened, it would disgorge rats into the soft underbelly of the Commons, and there would be nothing to stop them.

He stumbled backward in the darkness, his mouth as dry as sand.

He wheeled and flew back down the tunnel toward home.

◆ ◆ ◆

King SoSheth could not sleep. He stalked the downy carpet of his private chambers with the calculated movements of a caged tiger, quietly fuming.

He had sent the servants away. Normally he did not like to be alone. Being alone reminded him of his terrible and secret inadequacies. A king, after all, is not really much different from his subjects, though he may pretend otherwise. But just now he felt too angry to notice his loneliness.

Fear and fury warred in his mind. Who did this overgrown hangnail—this GoRec—think he was? What harm had Tira-Nor done to the rats to provoke such spite? What right did GoRec have to wrest SoSheth's city from him?

It had been half a day since GoRec had appeared at the West Gate with another challenge, but the words were branded white hot into SoSheth's brain. Nothing, it seemed, would erase them. The more he fretted, the hotter they burned.

"Mouse king," GoRec had shouted, the insolence in his voice palpable. "How long will you hide? Come. I will make you a new wager. Send me your best fighter. If he defeats me in fair battle, the rats of GoRec will leave Tira-Nor peacefully. If not, your vaunted kingsguard will fight us in the open for the prize of Tira-Nor!"

And what had King SoSheth done? Had he responded with dignity? With honor?

SoSheth scowled, his paws clenched into fists.

No. King SoSheth—renowned through the city as the ablest fighter in mouse history—had ordered Captain Blang to silence.

"Ignore the brute," JoHanan had said. "He is just taunting you."

Perhaps.

But how could SoSheth ignore the taunting of his own heart?

You abandoned ElShua. Now ElShua has abandoned you.

Truth was, he did fear GoRec. That admission—something he would never have confessed audibly—tormented him. Never mind that such fear made sense. GoRec was a monster, not a rat. Even the Ur'Lugh feared him.

The question was, Who *didn't* fear GoRec?

"Your Majesty," a voice said.

SoSheth turned, too startled to be angry.

A small mouse stood there, one of the kingsguard. He recognized the face. A shock of white fur drooped over one eye.

The tunnel-breaker. The serpent-killer. The one TaMir had anointed king over Tira-Nor. But this mouse certainly didn't look like a king. He didn't even look like one of the kingsguard. He was too small. Too young. Too humble.

"How did you get in here?" SoSheth demanded.

"Captain Blang gave his permission to the guards on duty. I told him I would wait until morning to speak to you, but then I heard you pacing, and I thought ..."

"I can't sleep. What of it?" SoSheth glared. After a moment he said more softly, "What do you want?"

"I ..." The tunnel-breaker looked away. In anyone else SoSheth would have assumed the pause expressed nervousness or fear of invoking his wrath. But the little mouse didn't seemed moved by either of these things.

"I don't have all night." A lie, of course. Who knew when he would sleep soundly again?

"Majesty," the little mouse said, his gaze on the matted floor. "I want permission to fight GoRec."

♦ ♦ ♦

HaRed wasted precious seconds bolting for home. He caught himself halfway back. A shadowy plan of rousing Mother and getting her to safety had wavered in his mind, but as he ran he realized this was impractical. The rats had to be stopped at the point of entry, or no place in Tira-Nor would be safe.

He stopped abruptly, turned, and hesitated a moment longer. There was, after all, only one place to go.

Moments later he stood outside the southernmost

barracks of the militia, where a guard stopped him in the entrance.

"What do you want?" the guard demanded.

"The rats are attacking."

The guard's eyes widened. "Where?"

"The southern perimeter."

"Are you sure? We've had no report of —"

"Yes, I'm sure," HaRed blurted. "How many reports do you need?"

To their credit, the militia — who were not as well trained as the kingsguard — responded quickly, though to HaRed it seemed to take forever to rouse the sleeping soldiers and form three quick-response squads.

HaRed was surprised the militia commanders only sent fifteen mice. When an officer ordered him to lead the foremost of the three five-mouse squads to where he had heard the borehole being dug, his feeling of impending doom grew. Quick-response squads were used like corks in a breaking dam and were considered expendable.

The squad leader, a civil engineer named MarSihlu, ordered the squad into a loose line while the other two squads were being roused. The plan, apparently, was to wait for the rats to complete the borehole and attack them as they fell through.

"All right," MarSihlu said. "It's time to earn our pay, such as it is. Lieutenant HuJeq doesn't think this is a serious threat. He thinks it's a feint. And who am I to argue with an officer?"

The squad laughed nervously.

"Nevertheless," MarSihlu continued, "if the rats get in, we could be in real trouble. Remember, they don't know the tunnels of the Commons the way we do. We're going to use that against them. Stay together. Watch your backs."

HaRed saw the terrible truth in his eyes. *These are not soldiers. They are common, ordinary mice. What chance do they have against trained rats?* When he understood how frightened they were, he stopped looking any of them in the eye.

MarSihlu drew himself up and looked from face to face. "Cheer up!" He smiled as if in demonstration. "I expect we'll all be back here before dawn, trying to sleep through FalKirq's snoring."

FalKirq grinned sheepishly, and again the mice laughed. MarSihlu's relaxed demeanor was helping, if only a little.

We're going to be too late, HaRed thought. King SoSheth had gambled everything on the assumption GoRec would attack the center, and now there were not enough defenders in position to save Tira-Nor. Not enough to save the Commons, anyway. The thought made him numb.

All his hopes. His bitterness and revenge. None of his plans would come to fruition. His life would be an absurd lesson in futility, with no one left to learn it. He had spent so many seasons lost in his self-importance, the truth of his own insignificance came as a shock. The realization washed like ice water over his heart, his mind.

But oddly, it came as a relief too. He felt as though he had been carrying himself on his shoulders, and all he had ever wanted was to just let go.

The two other squads formed in the chamber behind them.

"Ready?" MarSihlu said. "Follow me. Double time." He turned to HaRed. "Lead the way, soldier."

Soldier? The word carried connotations of ordinariness that HaRed should have resented. Instead, a strange sense of pride filled him.

"Yes, sir." It was the first time HaRed had ever used the word *sir* and really meant it.

He led them south toward the place where he had heard scratching a few moments before; the new borehole that was already spilling blood-frenzied rats into the poorest hovels of the Commons.

◆ ◆ ◆

"You are only a kit," King SoSheth said. "You cannot fight GoRec."

The runt drew himself up to his full height. "Majesty, I am a member of your own kingsguard, trained by General LaRish himself."

SoSheth pursed his lips.

"I fought at the battle of Dry Gully, Majesty." The runt's voice sounded oddly confident, as though death meant nothing to him. "I killed the snake in the Chamber of Wroth. This rat will be no different."

SoSheth sighed deeply and began to pace again as JaRed waited in silence for an answer. Tira-Nor could not resist the siege much longer. Though they had food for several weeks, they lacked water. Even at half-rations, it was a matter of days, not weeks, before the females and kits began to die. *Why didn't ElShua send rain?*

Something must be done, and soon. Perhaps the city should be evacuated, turned over to the rats in exchange for a promise of safe conduct. But could the rats be trusted?

No.

A late-night evacuation, then? Under cover of darkness, perhaps?

No.

So many females and kits in the Dark Forest would not survive. Even if they did, where would they go?

Curse all rats forever!

SoSheth was tired. So very tired. The weight of kingship hung heavily on his shoulders. Should they stay and die slowly, or leave and die quickly? Which was more merciful? Which more certain?

"Majesty."

Though soft, the interruption irritated him. "What?"

Runt lowered his gaze. "ElShua is with me."

SoSheth let out a long, slow breath. This was what SoSheth feared the most, that ElShua *was* with this tunnel-breaker, this serpent-killer, this JaRed son of ReDemec the Red.

Come to think of it, this was what had bothered the brother too. SoSheth had seen it in his eyes when he related TaMir's prophecy.

TaMir. Who had once been a friend. Who had spoken of ElShua's favor.

Well, where was ElShua now?

"It is *my* city," SoSheth said through clenched teeth.

"My lord?"

SoSheth spat. "It is my kingdom. Not GoRec's. Not yours. Not ElShua's. Mine!"

The runt retreated two steps, toward the shadows, a look of unbelief stitched across his face. It was a look SoSheth would never forget.

But then he saw the answer. Not an easy answer. But not a difficult one either.

It was obvious, really. King SoSheth had nothing to lose.

He would allow ReDemec's son to fight GoRec, and the runt would be killed. And while the Ur'Lugh cheered his death, King SoSheth would order the kingsguard to slide quietly out of the Royal, West, and Shade Gates and attack the rats in force. The kingsguard would have surprise on their side, if nothing else.

Perhaps, with much luck, they could collapse the rat center. And once that happened ... GoRec's army would turn to vapor without a strong leader.

Perhaps.

At least if Tira-Nor falls it will do so under me, not under this half-sized commoner.

SoSheth cleared his throat. "Are you certain?"

Runt looked up. "Yes, Majesty."

SoSheth nodded. "All right. I will tell my armorer to make you ready by morning. Captain Blang will advise GoRec that Tira-Nor has accepted his challenge. You will be our champion, JaRed son of ReDemec."

"Thank you, Majesty."

Thank you?

JaRed's tone told SoSheth that he knew his king was sending him to die, yet he did not draw back. The runt did not seem to carry the heaviness of a death sentence on his shoulders.

Odd. And what if he somehow survives? What then?

SoSheth clenched his teeth.

Then I will kill JaRed son of ReDemec the Red myself.

◆ ◆ ◆

HaRed took a stunning blow to the side of his head as he rounded the corner into the perimeter tunnel. The rat's claws dug into the side of his face, gouging four long lines into his cheek. The impact knocked him sideways into the far wall. He landed awkwardly on one shoulder, virtually upside down, his head spinning.

The tunnel narrowed, turned. He felt dizzy, and thought for a moment he would faint. He heard screams. In the distance, perhaps fifteen lengths away, the borehole opened in the tunnel ceiling. Rats poured through in a steady stream, jamming the tunnel near the hole as their eyes adjusted to the darkness.

MarSihlu leapt into the closest rat and went down in a blur of motion. Behind him, two of the five mice in his squad ran squealing from the fight.

Cowards.

The other three mice stepped nervously into the intersection to block the passage into the heart of Tira-Nor.

FalKirq, the one who snored, went down under the weight of a rat who came seemingly from nowhere.

HaRed tried to stand, but the world exploded as a brown wall of fur drove him headfirst into the tunnel floor. Pain seared his spine. He felt the hot breath of the rat on his skin just before it bit into his neck.

HaRed squirmed and twisted over onto his back. The rat kicked at HaRed's rump with his hind legs, but succeeded only in gouging his own tail.

White-hot rage consumed him in an instant and the pain dissipated. HaRed lunged upward and sank his own teeth into the rat's throat.

He wanted nothing more at that moment than to kill this horrible invader. And kill it he would. For his teeth were already drawing out the rat's lifeblood. It squirmed and writhed and struggled, but HaRed held on.

The other rats did not intervene in the fight. They flowed around him west and north along both tunnels.

MarSihlu died bravely, amid a torrent of blows from three rats who teamed up to kill the obvious leader of the squad. The two remaining militia-mice kept their heads. They backed slowly into the intersecting tunnel and made their stand side by side. They dispatched two rats and wounded a third before succumbing to the rats' superior size and skill.

Their stand did not last long, but it was long enough. Behind them, the second and third quick-response squads piled into the tunnel and began pushing the rats back towards the perimeter.

HaRed saw his chance. He never had been brave. Only clever. Ironically, at that moment, bravery found him.

He saw the temporary retreat of the rats from the intersecting tunnel and realized what would happen next.

Rats still poured in from the borehole. The perimeter tunnel stood packed with two or three dozen invaders. The pressure of the rats pushing both direc-

tions down the tunnel prevented those at the intersection from retreating toward the borehole. Instead,
the overflow of sweating, cursing invaders flowed the
other direction. The rats were running west along the
perimeter. Already at least six or seven had gone that
way. Eventually they would find the next intersecting
tunnel, and the invasion would be that much harder to
contain.

The next intersection was not far. The rats may have
found it already.

HaRed picked himself up and ran.

Ahead, he heard the sneering, cursing, and laughing of rats as they nosed the walls, the floor. Behind
him, he heard more rats.

They all ran in darkness now. There were no glowstones within fifty lengths, and those were concealed
by turns and double-backs.

They had come to the perimeter defenses of the
Wind Gate. The double-backs, maze hatches, fools'
errands, and wall stones on which King SoSheth was
apparently depending. HaRed remembered what Mar-
Sihlu had said. *The rats don't know the tunnels of the Commons the way we do. We're going to use that against them.*

Indeed.

There were two holes in Tira-Nor's defenses: two
tunnels by which the rats were stumbling into the city.
If he could plug at least one of them, the kingsguard
would stand a chance. He would cut off the westward
flow of rats down the perimeter.

HaRed pressed himself against one wall, feeling
his way forward. He had picked an opportune time to
follow. Between the rats up ahead and the rats some

distance behind he found a gap of silent emptiness that meant safety.

But some of the invaders had already gone down the western passage, and after he blocked the tunnel, they would still be inside Tira-Nor's defenseless Commons. While he was blocking the passage, where would these attackers go?

HaRed knew, and the knowledge congealed into a lump of despair so real that for a moment he stood frozen by indecision.

Whose home lay closest to the Wind Gate? Whose home boasted of the southernmost chambers of Tira-Nor?

Father's. The home of ReDemec the Red, where Mother lay asleep even now, unaware of the danger sniffing and gnawing its way toward her.

He couldn't leave her alone. Could he?

But if the passage weren't blocked, there would soon be so many rats inside Tira-Nor that nothing could protect any of the mice. All of them would die, including Mother.

He made his decision, and for the first time in many seasons felt the hot sting of tears streaming down his cheek. The tears burned as they hit the long gashes left there by a rat's claws.

He sprang forward, his paws padding the earth in the darkness until he came to the almost imperceptible dip in the ground.

HaRed stopped and turned to his right. He stood on his hind legs, feeling for the opening. The world spun, and he was forced to rest. He had lost too much blood. The blow to his head had done more damage

than he realized. Yet Tira-Nor could not afford for him
to lose consciousness.

The rats that had followed him drew closer, their
voices now distinct in the darkness.

"Whole place stinks of mice," one of them said.

"Reeks," said another.

He shook his head to clear it and reached up again
in the blackness. He found the high, hidden ledge and
leapt upward, scrabbling in the darkness, his paws
kicking against the packed dirt of the tunnel wall. His
body shook and a cold sweat broke out on his forehead.

I'm going to die here.

"What's that?" a rat snarled. "Up ahead there. You
hear something?"

"I didn't hear nothin'."

HaRed pushed into the black emptiness of the
cave-like alcove, one paw on the smooth stone that
was perched just above the tunnel. The trap was meant
to seal off the Wind Gate, in case it ever fell into the
hands of invaders. But it would just as effectively block
anyone from coming the other direction into the gate
complex ... and from there into Tira-Nor.

He felt along the dirt wall until he found the thick
shaft of wood that was jammed into retaining stones
on either side of a long lever. He had only to slide the
shaft out from under one retainer. The lever would
snap upward and the wall stone would drop into the
mouth of the tunnel.

The engineers called these devices *snake eggs*
because the stones—which were actually larger than
the tunnel itself—were supposed to fit like an egg in a
snake's belly.

For just a moment he hesitated. Then he reached forward and shoved.

The lever didn't budge.

He pushed again.

Impossible!

How many days had he contemplated tripping the lever out of pure spite? How many times had he rested a paw against the same shaft of wood, certain a simple nudge would bring the world crashing down on the tunnel? And now that there was a cause, it wouldn't move!

HaRed glared into the darkness. He licked his lips and pushed again, even harder.

The lever was stuck fast, and HaRed had no strength left. His body had betrayed him. It had betrayed all of Tira-Nor.

He closed his eyes to keep the world from spinning, then braced his rear legs against the dirt wall behind him. He stretched out both front paws to grasp the lever, knowing the effort was beyond him now.

Without thinking about what he was doing, he whispered, "Please. Help me."

He shoved a third time, and fireworks exploded behind his eyes. Something cracked, and the lever slipped forward. His arms slipped down the shaft and he landed face first on the floor.

Above, the stone groaned softly, then thudded downward in its groves.

Several rats were approaching in the tunnel below. The noise and thunder of the falling stone must have awakened their blackest fears. They seemed to think all the Earth was collapsing around them. They turned and fled, screaming murder and death and the end of the world.

HaRed closed his eyes and waited for death to come.

◆ ◆ ◆

When HaRed awoke he could not tell how long he had been unconscious. His neck ached and his throat burned with thirst. The blood on his cheek had caked into four long scabs. He marveled that he was still alive.

He stood on wobbly legs and slid gingerly back down into the tunnel. He could not take the western route home to find out what had happened to Mother, Merry, and Berry. He stood now on the wrong side of the stone. He would have to go the long way, through the mass of rats. If they were still there.

And what if Tira-Nor had already fallen?

Well, he would kill one or two more rats before the day was over. *Come and get me.*

There were no sounds of fighting from the intersection up ahead, but he could see by the blue-misted haze of light from the nearest glowstone that many bodies lay in the tunnel.

The battle had ended, but only recently. He must not have been unconscious very long.

The mice of the quick-response squads were all dead. He recognized their faces, the faces of the soldiers who had followed him.

Soldiers. That word did not sound ordinary now. It would never sound ordinary again.

They had saved Tira-Nor, at least for a few hours. They had plugged the dam just long enough for the kingsguard to arrive from their posts at the Wind and Forest garrisons. Kingsguard warriors moved in the distance.

HaRed passed body after body. More than thirty mice, and almost as many rats, lay unmoving in the tunnel. The wounded groaned quietly, their backs propped against the wall. Many of them would die before the night was over. For these he felt genuine pity.

When he came to the intersection, HaRed saw the borehole was now clear of rats. A tight circle of kings-guard warriors crowded around the pale ribbon of moonlight that stabbed the darkness from the hole.

"Engineers," Lieutenant KoVeek snapped. "I want engineers here in twenty heartbeats. I want this entire section of tunnel collapsed!"

One of the kingsguard saluted. "I'll see to it."

KoVeek saw HaRed and his eyes narrowed. "What are you doing here?"

"My name is HaRed son of ReDemec the Red. I was part of the militia that responded to the rat's attack. I tripped the wall stone."

KoVeek nodded. "Well done."

"Please. There were other rats on the far side of the stone. I must find out about my family."

"ReDemec the Red, you say?" KoVeek glanced sideways toward one of his sergeants, who whispered something in his ear.

"Yes. Very well. Sergeant PoTeesh will go with you. He has just come from there."

The sergeant saluted Lieutenant KoVeek and approached HaRed, limping from a gash in his right hind leg. "HaRed," the sergeant said as they walked, "I hate to tell you this, but there is a reason the lieutenant sent me with you. My squad ran into eight rats who were looting in the southwest quadrant of the Wind section."

The lump in HaRed's throat tightened. "What are you trying to tell me?"

"You have some nasty wounds, HaRed. You should walk, not run."

HaRed had already broken into a steady trot, the fastest pace he could manage. And the injured sergeant could not keep up with him.

From behind him the sergeant called out, "It's too late for them, HaRed!"

◆ ◆ ◆

King SoSheth's armorer led JaRed into the private armory of the king just before dawn.

"You have your choice of oils," the armorer said. His voice lacked confidence, and his eyes revealed a pity JaRed resented.

JaRed shook his head. "I'm not used to being oiled. It would only hinder me."

The armorer shrugged. "I was ordered to give you anything you asked for."

"Good. In that case, I need you to go back to the barracks where I keep my things …"

◆ ◆ ◆

HaRed saw the rats first. Their deaths had been swift and efficient. The work of the kingsguard.

Then he saw Merry and Berry.

They lay dead outside the entrance to the family chambers. He placed one paw aside each neck. No pulse, though the skin was still warm.

Inside, in the darkness of the entrance, he called, "Mother?"

"HaRed?" Her voice came faintly, with a gasp.

"Mother?" In the darkness it took him a moment to find her. She lay on the floor. He cradled her head in his paws.

Blue-green light flooded the room. Sergeant PoTeesh stood in the entry, holding a glowstone. "I thought you might want—" When he saw HaRed's mother he stopped mid-sentence.

"HaRed," Mother said, "you're safe. Where are Merry and Berry?"

"They're ... safe too," HaRed whispered. "Don't talk."

"You fought them, didn't you?" Mother said.

HaRed glanced down, saw her wounds, and gulped. Fresh tears spilled down his cheek. "Don't talk, Mother."

"HaRed. My favorite son."

HaRed blinked. He wasn't Mother's favorite. *Runt* was.

"Do you know why you were always my favorite? It's because you are so much like me. I understand you. Never good enough. Never the oldest. Never the strongest. I'm sorry you must carry my weaknesses. But one day long ago I learned what really matters in life. Do you know what it is, HaRed?" Her eyes widened a moment and glistened as she smiled. "You do, don't you? I can see it in you now."

HaRed didn't understand. He didn't even know if anything mattered. But she seemed so sure, and she seemed to want him to be sure too. He nodded.

"I'm thirsty."

"I'll get you something." He started to stand but she stopped him, gripping his arm weakly.

"It's all right, HaRed. Tell Papa … and KahEesha. Tell JaRed …" She looked past him toward the ceiling. "Oh, HaRed, I hear his wings! Do you hear them?"

HaRed heard nothing, but he nodded anyway. "I hear them, Mother. He comes gently for you."

"Tell JaRed —"

Then her breath spilled out and she said nothing more.

Chapter Eleven

GoRec

Shift. Look. Step.

"Tweener!"

Use your eyes, leetle one. Look! The Earth is dying, yes?

It was true. The Earth was dying. Shuddering under the impact of a weight larger than it could bear. Convulsing like some giant beast in the final moments of its life. Crumbling. Falling away beneath him. Collapsing into a perfect black hole of nothingness.

Shift — boom!

Look — boom!

Step—boom!

It rattled and shook, as though crushed under some monstrous weight. ElShua's footsteps on the crust of the world.

Boom!

Or were they Wroth's footsteps?

JaRed could not tell. He could not see through the dim fog of the vision. The only clear thing was the sense of weightlessness, of smallness, of having no firm grip on anything.

"Tweener!" A voice like the coming of doom fell from the sky.

Then, suddenly, JaRed could see. He couldn't help but see. Towering above even the clouds, a giant rat, its mouth foaming pink, its eyes rolled back into its head until only the blood-veined white showed.

GoRec!

Shift—Boom!

"Tweener has come," boomed the rat. Its voice battered JaRed's ears, hammered at his brain.

It occurred to him that he did not have to fall into the black hole. Did not have to descend into the emptiness. Did not have to die with the world. He could just slip away. Disappear. Make himself invisible and flee into the Dark Forest.

And why not?

King SoSheth hates me. Horrid hates me. LaRish is dead. There's nothing left for me here. Nothing left to live for. Nothing left to die for.

Why *not* run away?

A plan emerged. He would slide out through the Mud Gate just before dawn. He would weave his way past the rat siege lines. He would fade into the shadows of the trees and lose himself in the coolness of the wood. Even if one of the rat sentries saw him, he would not pursue him far. Not with the rest of Tira-Nor still to deal with. Besides, even if they wanted to, the rats could not catch him. They were too slow.

GoRec's eyes rolled forward, revealing the black marble void that filled them. "And then what?" His voice echoed in the black, silent chamber. It rolled off the walls like water and hurled itself in waves against JaRed. Even as it subsided it lost none of its power. It scratched at his eyes, softer, though still insistent, searching. "And then what?"

Eh, leetle one? What would it be like in the Dark Forest without purpose? Without meaning?

"JaRed?"

He looked up into the blue haze of a glowstone shining somewhere in the distance down the tunnel. TaMir stood rimmed in light at the entrance, his enormous white body a shadowy silhouette.

JaRed remembered. He knelt on the dirt floor of his chamber in the officer's section of the kingsguard He had come here to be alone, but had found he could not control his own thoughts. Slowly, a vast blanket of terror had settled around him, suffocating him, until peace had seemed nothing but a distant memory. *Where are you?*

Then the vision. So real. The Earth dying, and GoRec towering above the heavens.

TaMir cleared his throat. "And then what?"

JaRed blinked. "TaMir?"

"After you flee," the seer said. "Then what will happen?"

JaRed swallowed and looked away. "I saw GoRec in a vision. His paws were crushing the life out of the whole world."

TaMir sighed and shuffled into the room. "He would do that if he could." He grimaced and put one paw to his lower back. He sat next to JaRed and leaned stiffly against the wall of the chamber, exhaling with a sound like the winter wind. "Perhaps that *would* happen were you to leave Tira-Nor to its own fate."

"Perhaps?"

"Or perhaps Tira-Nor will fall no matter what you do. That is a possibility I have long considered. But I do not believe it. In my bones I believe you were born to make a difference."

"But … you're a seer. You already know the future."

TaMir laughed, his voice rattling dryly in the cool stillness of the chamber. "I know very little. And what I do know comes from the past, not the future. Oh, yes, sometimes ElShua whispers a riddle in my ear. Once in a great while He may give me a hint about what will happen. But He does not tell me *how*. And the *how*, dear JaRed, is the thing that gives life color."

JaRed shook his head. "I don't understand."

TaMir nodded slowly. "Neither do I. But then, in the end, understanding is not really all that important."

"No?"

"No."

"I wish I could believe that."

TaMir's brows furrowed. His eyes glimmered in the wispy light. An expression of sympathy etched his face. "What is it, JaRed?"

"What is *what*?"

"The thing that bothers you. It is more than fear of GoRec, or fear of death. You have wanted to ask me something. All night you have battled in your heart. I can see the pain of it written on your face. An unanswered question troubles you. Isn't that why I am here? Ask it."

JaRed swallowed. He felt grateful, but also afraid. For what if the answer were some deficiency in himself? What if the answer was worse than the question? "Why does ElShua seem so far away?" he asked, and the weight of it fell from him.

TaMir's shoulders slumped, as though with grief, and he let out a long, slow breath.

JaRed wondered whether TaMir had fallen asleep, or was offended, or simply had no answer, because it was a long time before the seer spoke.

"Because," TaMir said in a voice as far away as a dream, "he wants to trust you, JaRed. It is an opportunity. A chance to shine. Even Wroth can be forced to behave in ElShua's presence. It is what one does in his absence that reveals one's heart." He reached over and patted JaRed's paw. "When the time comes, I think you will discover he has never left you."

"I'd like to believe that. It's just ..."

TaMir smiled. "Then I should like to tell you a story. Did you know you are not the first mouse to have been anointed king over Tira-Nor? No? Nor are you the first to feel unworthy of the calling.

"There was a mouse, some time ago, who was called to great things, much like you. He too faced a mighty army of rats. This mouse was given the opportunity of a lifetime: the chance to lean upon ElShua instead of himself. But when the whisper of the Maker came, and the king was told *not* to attack, but to wait ... well, this mouse disobeyed. Instead of heeding ElShua's command, he took the matter into his own paws. He attacked what he thought was a weakness in the rat line. Because ElShua seemed far off."

"What happened?"

"Many mice died. The king was rejected, and another mouse was appointed in his place a few years later."

"I see."

TaMir's gaze flicked over to him. "Do you?"

JaRed cocked his head. "Well, yes. I mean, I think so. The king doubted and disobeyed. And he paid a very high price for not doing what he should have done."

TaMir pursed his lips and nodded gently, as though unimpressed by JaRed's answer. "Yes, yes. That is almost it. The king lived a long time, you see. He tried to forget, to pretend the responsibility of so many deaths lay with others. He blamed his advisors. His general. He even blamed ElShua."

JaRed gasped.

"But that doesn't work, does it?"

JaRed stared at the old mouse in disbelief, his mouth open.

"Ah," said TaMir. "Now you see."

"You're talking about SoSheth," JaRed blurted. "He is the king in your story."

"Yes."

"And I am the one who was chosen to take his place."

TaMir nodded. "Yes. LaRish was the general. I, one of the advisors."

They sat in silence for a long time, neither one speaking. It seemed, for a while, they had all the time in the world, that the only thing that mattered was to sit quietly and listen to the distant sounds of the kingsguard coming to life in the early moments before dawn.

"Does it hurt?" JaRed whispered finally, his voice as thin as the light beyond the door.

"Does what hurt?" TaMir asked. "Dying?"

"No. Growing old."

TaMir's lips pursed. His mouth opened and closed soundlessly. At last he said, "It is the memories that hurt the most." He reached down with one paw and rubbed the swollen mound of his left knee. "But in the end, you either enter ElShua's garden wounded, or you do not enter it at all."

◆ ◆ ◆

"Well, mouse," GoRec called from above. His voice boomed in the underground chambers, echoing like thunder in the gray haze. "Have you changed your mind?"

HaRed waited in silence, the words piercing his heart. Even here in the Great Hall, GoRec's voice could be clearly heard, resounding down the long tunnel that led from the Common Gate. Here, surrounded by what seemed half the Commons, HaRed felt utterly alone. He did not know—or would not admit—what bothered him. He reached up with one paw and picked at the long scabs on his cheek, as though by removing them he could remove the scars from his soul.

The mice of the Commons waited. Everyone knew what was happening. Runt of the kingsguard — *Runt the Brave*, some had called him — was about to be killed by the monster rat, GoRec. Then Tira-Nor's kingsguard and militia would spill from their positions and attack in force while the females and kits fled toward the Dark Forest from the five easternmost gates. This was SoSheth's plan.

Not a good plan, but what choice did they have? There wasn't enough water for Tira-Nor to hold out any longer.

HaRed swallowed the lump in his throat. *It would serve the little waste-of-air right, really.* But this spite somehow came reluctantly. *Runt the brave?* he thought. *No, not him!*

HaRed tried to work up enough saliva in his throat for a good spit, but failed.

Yes. JaRed was brave.

HaRed marveled that he had allowed himself to admit such a thought.

The Great Hall stank of too many mice. Too much sweat, too much anxiety, too much thirst.

He took a long pull of the heavy air and licked his lips. His tongue felt like sand. Everything was drying out. Leaking moisture into the dry autumn air.

Even his hatred for JaRed was draining away. It poured from his heart like blood from an old wound.

Old. And self-inflicted.

HaRed swallowed again, but the thirst would not leave him. How long would it take for JaRed to die? HaRed was not in a position to see the fight. He would not even see JaRed leaving the city. His brother would be going out from the West Gate any moment. HaRed expected to hear jeers from the rats.

The silence lingered. HaRed shifted his weight from one side to another. He had been posted to the militia here in the Great Hall along with several hundred other sudden-soldiers who now stood in hushed expectation. He did not mind their company. It seemed fitting, somehow, though he wished he could have spent his last day with one of the mice from the quick-response squads who had been sacrificed for a day of freedom.

My brother is about to die.

HaRed tried again to swallow. The knot in his throat seemed larger now, more demanding.

And I will die too.

But HaRed was Mother's favorite. She'd said so. And there was no denying the expression of love on her face just before she died. "Tell JaRed." she had said.

Tell him what?

A sound like rain erupted from the tunnel, the sound of cheering from the Ur'Lugh up above.

"Runt's gone out," someone said, as though it were not obvious.

From a few lengths away, a different mouse said, "Well, one less mouse to drink our water."

Something inside HaRed shattered at the impact of those words. His hatred exploded like black ice under a sledge.

My brother is about to die.

A fury he had never known erupted in his heart, and he wheeled about suddenly, causing those around him to shrink back. "Who said that?"

Silence.

"Who said that!" he shrieked.

The mice nearest him backed away, leaving him in a growing circle of emptiness.

"Answer me, coward!"

HaRed son of ReDemec the Red looked from face to face, his eyes wild, his throat hoarse, his cheek running with blood from a freshly peeled scab. But the lump in his throat was gone, driven out by the force of his anger.

"JaRed is my brother!" The Great Hall echoed with his rage. "Show yourself. I'll rip you apart piece by piece!"

But no one answered him.

◆ ◆ ◆

Captain Blang put one paw on JaRed's shoulder and whispered in his ear.

"Really?" JaRed said. Morning light from the West Gate burned brightly in the mouth of the tunnel. He could smell the rats outside, waiting.

"Yes. I asked her yesterday. I'd like you to attend."

"All right."

King SoSheth nosed into the crowded guard room with JoHanan and the royal escort. Both wore a heavy coat of oil. "Well, JaRed, are you ready?"

"Yes, Majesty."

"You honor us by your courage."

"Thank you, Majesty."

King SoSheth smiled thinly.

JoHanan came closer. "How's the shoulder? Any better?"

"I can manage."

"JaRed," JoHanan said, his voice soft, "are you sure you know what you're doing?"

Resentment flooded through him. It was irrational, he knew. JoHanan cared about him. Really and truly cared. And yet they all assumed he was about to die. Had they no hope? No faith?

"What do you think?" His voice rose as he spoke. "Do you really believe a sewage-eating rat can stand against the people of ElShua? We were given Tira-Nor. We have a covenant with the Maker. Who is this bald-tailed servant of Wroth?"

The others in the room looked around uncomfortably, and JaRed saw his words had not helped them at all. He saw the truth on their faces.

They don't believe. Not really. They think we are alone. They think the universe is an accident. They think GoRec will win and all of us will be dead by tomorrow.

Yet his words had affected himself.

If I die, then life is pointless anyway, for it will mean that all I believe is a lie: ElShua, Tira-Nor, the Garden Beyond. Nothing will have mattered.

So I would rather die with purpose than live with despair.

He padded out of the crowded guardroom and up the tunnel, followed closely by the king and Captain Blang.

"JaRed," Blang said.

JaRed turned.

"I watched LaRish fight that monster. After he raises up, he usually strikes from the left." Captain Blang moved his head from side to side in demonstration. "Right-left-right, then a left strike." He shrugged. "I just thought you should know."

JaRed nodded, then took the last few steps alone, dragging the ten-penny nail behind him. The other mice did not speak, though each no doubt wondered what he intended to do with the iron stick.

JaRed stepped forward and stood blinking in the wide-open sunlight of morning.

◆ ◆ ◆

JaRed knew the death match would be a game to GoRec, just as watching JaRed drag LaRish's body had been a game to him. True to his word, though probably not because of it, the rat had ordered the Ur'Lugh into a wide semicircle behind him. It was to be, as promised, "a fair fight."

As JaRed stepped forward, a scowl crept slowly over GoRec's face. "Where is your champion? When is he coming?"

In the brightness of the prairie, the full magnitude of his own vulnerability struck JaRed like a fist. He had nowhere to hide now. His ability to conceal himself would do him no good here. For the first time in his life, all attention was focused on him. He could not blend into the greenery or fade into the background.

Yet wasn't this what he had always wanted? To be noticed? To be considered important? To matter?

I've been a fool. Esteem won't make me great. It is only another snake in a dark tunnel waiting to devour me.

A shadow passed across the sun, and JaRed looked up into the cloudless sky. A hawk circled there, too far away to be distinct.

Hawks don't cast shadows at that distance. He thrust the thought from his mind. It didn't matter now.

"I am the champion of Tira-Nor," he said.

After a short pause, the Ur'Lugh jeered. They pointed, clapped one another's backs, and shook their heads in disbelief. Their derision fell like rain.

JaRed drew himself up and inched closer. Truly, GoRec the rat was huge.

The shadow passed again, and JaRed looked up. The rats did not seem to notice, which struck JaRed as odd.

A cold shiver raced down his spine as he stared heavenward. The bird circling overhead was no hawk. It was an owl. It slid through the sky as silent as the wind, its snow-white wings spread in a graceful half-moon. Gliding closer.

It has come for me. And perhaps for many others.

He stood staring at it, speechless, wondering again where the presence of ElShua had gone, wondering why he felt nothing but a cold tingle at his spine, as though death were clutching at him, rising from the earth with icy fingers.

GoRec sneered. "Am I a mouse, that the king of Tira-Nor sends a flea to bite me? What is the meaning of this insult?"

JaRed looked from face to sneering face. Fear coursed through his limbs, and he wondered if they could see that he was shaking. He forced himself to stand straight anyway. "You want to know why I was chosen to fight you? Very well. Here is the meaning, rat. I am here to show you that might does not make right."

There was a pause, followed by another, even louder round of laughter. Only GoRec didn't join in.

JaRed stood just beyond GoRec's reach. "Hear me, rats of GoRec," he said, pretending a confidence he did not feel. "And remember my words when your master dies at my teeth. ElShua is lord of the mice, lord of the rats, lord even of the Great Owl. Lord Wroth is nothing. I spit on him."

JaRed spat for emphasis, though nothing came out. His mouth felt dry as dust.

"Your teeth?" GoRec's face twisted into a sneer. "Teeth on a flea?"

"Yes," JaRed said so quietly that only GoRec could hear. The nail still felt cool in his paw, though GoRec had not seemed to notice it. "You are about to be killed by a mouse called *Runt*."

GoRec leapt forward, hissing, one paw raised in a white blur of motion.

One instant the long, black claws were held up like curved daggers. The next instant they sliced wickedly at JaRed's throat.

JaRed ducked, twisting sideways and backward to avoid the blow.

GoRec's open jaws filled JaRed's vision: the long, fox-like teeth, the black-spotted tongue, the rotting gums.

Then, before any time at all seemed to have passed, the jaws closed. The gums and tongue disappeared. Spittle flew in great glittering droplets that hung suspended in the air. The yellow canines slammed shut on JaRed's outstretched arm.

But JaRed's arm was no longer there. In the flash-motion timelessness of battle, he had slipped under GoRec's chin and withdrawn into a defensive fighting stance.

GoRec's body moved like a rope, looping around and through itself in effortless circles as he drove JaRed backward, sideways, down. He came with an unrelenting flurry of slashes, kicks, and bites. His movements were ghostlike: silent, fluid, untraceable. His lips curled back in a doglike growl as he spewed a torrent of foul breath and even fouler curses.

On and on he came, hurling himself at JaRed like a meteor.

Somehow JaRed evaded every blow, though only by a hair's breadth. For a long time he barely managed to follow the endless stream of GoRec's attack, concentrating solely on his own survival. He still gripped the nail, but he could not use it. He saw no opening in the rat's defenses. The nail grew heavier as JaRed ducked, twisted, evaded.

Blow after blow thudded past. Strike after strike hammered the air. Bite after bite narrowly missed.

Eventually GoRec seemed to realize the mouse he fought was too fast to be killed the way he killed other mice and rats. He changed tactics. He made shorter strikes, tried to simply grab JaRed with an open paw.

GoRec was using his weight now, trying to force an opening so he could pin JaRed rather than pummel him. JaRed knew what would happen if the monster upended him. Claws to the belly.

A slow, agonizing death.

JaRed saw the opening briefly, but was so shocked he didn't have time to take advantage of it. GoRec spread his front paws, struck downward with his teeth like a viper. He lashed out with his hind legs, struck the air with his coiling tail.

JaRed whirled, leapt, ducked.

Back and forth they moved across the earth, their breath coming in great heaves, sweat pouring from their flesh.

The Ur'Lugh stood like a line of statues, staring grim-faced in disbelief, their enthusiastic cheers now silent.

In a flash, JaRed recalled Blang's warning. *He usually strikes from the left. Right-left-right, then a left strike.*

But this missed the point. JaRed remembered GoRec's fight at the burn pile. It was not the angle that mattered, but the moment.

GoRec always struck after three feints.

To JaRed it seemed the fight expanded into a larger container, as though time had slowed to a crawl.

GoRec moved right, then left, then right again. When he lunged forward, JaRed heaved the rusting point of the nail in a silver-tipped arc, praying as he did so. The nail cut the air, whistling as it sliced toward GoRec's throat.

JaRed felt the sudden, jarring impact as the point struck home.

GoRec hesitated, tottered. A scowl of confusion twisted his face. He gripped the shaft of the nail with one paw.

He smiled grimly. "What's this?" GoRec pulled the point of the nail away from his throat, JaRed still gripping the other end. "A mouse fang?"

A trickle of blood ran from a point on GoRec's neck

just above his chest. Enough to make him angry, and no more. A mosquito bite, not a death strike.

GoRec ripped the nail out of JaRed's grasp with an effortless twist and cast it away.

The Ur'Lugh cheered.

A cold chill swept through JaRed's body, though sweat still poured down his face. Despair, heavier than any nail, settled on his shoulders. He clenched his teeth.

So, we are alone after all.

The world began to tilt, to slide away like some great table spilling its contents over the edge of the horizon.

"Hear me, mice of Tira-Nor," GoRec said, his voice raised in triumph. "And know that GoRec is master of the universe!" The emptiness of his black and lifeless eyes filled with a consuming hatred.

"What did they do to you?" JaRed asked. He did not know where the words came from.

GoRec hesitated, though he did not relax. "They are mice," he said, as though that were explanation enough.

JaRed shook his head. "Not the mice of Tira-Nor. I mean the mice of your past. The ones who used to torment you when you were small. Before you made your bargain with Lord Wroth."

GoRec's eyes opened wide.

"*Those* are the mice you hate. The Meatsies. The Dumpsters. The ones who knew you as Tweener. But why do you hate them? What did they do?"

GoRec seemed to shrink before him. Slowly, like water spilling from a drain, the hate emptied and the eyes glossed over. In that moment JaRed knew his vision had been true.

"Tweener," GoRec muttered, as though remembering something long forgotten. "The mice of the city dump. The mice of the meat-packaging plant. Yes. I knew them once. They were—" He looked around, as though coming to himself.

Compassion settled on JaRed's soul like a blanket. Hope erupted in his heart. Perhaps even GoRec was not beyond redemption. The thought shook him to the core, yet it brought an odd sensation of joy, of promise.

He stepped backward and looked over one shoulder at the sun-blasted earth that shrouded his city. Tira-Nor. City of Promise.

My city? Yes. My city and my people.

"They were *what*?" JaRed asked. "Cruel? Stupid? Thoughtless?"

"Yes." GoRec's eyes narrowed, and his gaze became malicious again. "They were cruel, stupid, thoughtless *mice*."

Without warning, GoRec lunged forward, reaching with outstretched paws.

JaRed stepped back and twisted away, scrambling for time. He needed to recover find his battle-mind, which had been lost in the moment of his vision.

He felt a tug at his ankle. An awkward yank.

No. This isn't supposed to—

The ground rose up like a wall and slammed into his face. Pain exploded behind his eyes. Fingers of light splintered his brain.

He did not see which of the Ur'Lugh had reached into the open arena to trip him. But he heard the resulting cheers.

He shoved against the earth, against the blinding pain and blackness. He raised himself to all fours and wobbled there unsteadily. He tasted blood in his mouth. Blood and dirt.

He blinked, trying to focus. The world shivered under a cloak of gray mist. The sun dimmed behind a thick, blood-red veil. The sky swayed heavily above him.

Who but the Owl could blot the sun so completely?

He reached out with both hands to steady himself, and his fingers brushed the head of the fallen nail. Then his back legs were circled in an iron grip and he was jerked backward. The world spun as his body was flipped over.

The back of his head struck the ground, felt as though it had burst open.

Agony. An ice-pick stabbing fire into the base of his skull.

He lay on his back, unable to breathe, blinking against the darkness and fear. He reached out with one arm and held the other aloft, as though to ward off the final descent of the Owl, who must even now be coming for him.

GoRec stood above him. One massive leg jammed into JaRed's stomach, the claws digging into JaRed's belly like razors. The rat held up his front paws and grinned, as if in demonstration that the fight had taken no effort at all.

"Yes," GoRec snarled. "My tormentors were mice. What other reason do I need for killing them? Or for killing you?"

The roar of the Ur'Lugh was thunderous.

JaRed reached back still farther, unable to see, but knowing it must be there, grasping desperately, his fingers clawing dirt, grass, empty air.

GoRec was toying with him, swaying above him like a pendulum. The face of death coming closer with each pass.

Noise and thunder. A deafening roar of Ur'Lugh voices. Cheering. Screaming. Laughing.

Death wears the face of a rat. He shuddered.

His fingers closed around the cool shaft of the nail, the ridges near the flat surface at the end.

The darkness split with a blinding light as the sun appeared behind GoRec's leering face. Then darkness again. Followed by light. The monster wavered. Right. Left. Right.

Now!

JaRed heaved on the shaft and raised the nail Its iron point stabbed upward like a pike its head braced against the earth to absorb the impact of GoRec's lightning attack.

He was too late.

He had underestimated the great brute's speed.

GoRec's weight crashed onto him. Death gave a great sigh and closed its teeth around JaRed's shoulder.

Far above them, unseen by anyone but JaRed, the Great Owl swooped.

◆ ◆ ◆

Captain Blang watched the battle silently from his perch high above the skirmish. To the south, Lieutenant KoVeek's detachment had deployed in a narrow

V aimed at the heart of the Ur'Lugh. As yet none of the rat officers seemed to notice Tira-Nor's kingsguard sliding out of both west-facing gates.

JaRed had drawn the rat in. Made himself seem vulnerable and small. Yet his speed was precise. His movements effortless. His limbs always just beyond reach, yet close enough to strike.

A young LaRish, Blang thought. Faster even than SoSheth used to be, when the king was in his prime.

There had been a moment during the fight when it seemed JaRed had accomplished the impossible. But his hidden skill had not been enough, for the nail had not pierced the rat's neck.

Instead, GoRec had pinned him. From this angle, Blang could not see how the killing was done. But he saw the side-to-side motion. The strike. The death blow had come. The fight was over.

JaRed had died bravely.

And now it was time. Captain Blang gave the signal, then leapt down the slope and into the line of the Ur'Lugh, followed closely by forty of his most skilled fighters.

He would avenge JaRed's death. LaRish's death. The death of his father, who died without a whimper.

Once the battle had begun, there was no time for memories. Only raking claws and slicing teeth. Evasion and attack. The terrible, heart-pounding beauty of his assault.

This was a blessing, for at last Captain Blang could release the pent-up rage he had hidden for so long. At last he could exact vengeance for the shame and suffering of childhood, of life.

In battle he could lose the awareness of what he was. A mouse. A rat-hater.

A *Dumpster*.

◆ ◆ ◆

JaRed struggled to raise the heavy, sweat-drenched rat off his chest. The nail bore some of the monster's weight, or JaRed would never have managed it.

The nail had entered GoRec's chest between two ribs, driven deep by his own size and speed as he struck downward to kill JaRed. The rat's mouth had opened reflexively, and his teeth had scraped the fur around JaRed's wounded shoulder.

JaRed twisted and shoved against the massive bulk, pulling his legs free as GoRec's body rolled sideways. He emerged just as Captain Blang and his warriors hit the Ur'Lugh line from the West Gate.

JaRed drew the nail from GoRec's chest and held it skyward, its shaft bloody and gleaming in the morning sun.

◆ ◆ ◆

The mice of Tira-Nor believe what happened next was the fault of the rats themselves. GoRec's followers had placed so much hope in him they didn't know what to do when he was gone. Their stories about him, though preposterous, were nonetheless believed, and this made his death all the more impossible. GoRec, after all, was Lord Wroth's own stepchild. GoRec would live forever. He would lead the rats to victory over the mice of Tira-Nor, over the mice of the whole world. GoRec could not be defeated by mortal flesh. Anything that killed GoRec would have to be a ghost, or a demon, or a wraith from the blackest pits of the earth.

One could hardly blame the rats for their fear. From the moment JaRed appeared victorious on the battle-field, an aura surrounded him, a mystique of invulnerability. As he shoved GoRec's body aside and held up the nail, he seemed — to some of the rats — to have passed ghost-like all the way through GoRec's body.

Then, too, the rats, being clever only in evil, could not comprehend the simplicity of the killing. It seemed to them JaRed had grown a fang from his paw. No doubt this was why some of them believed the mouse fiend who killed their master was able to change him-self into a giant snake.

Leaderless, the rats found themselves at the mercy of the very thing that had driven them to attack Tira-Nor. Fear. With GoRec gone, the Ur'Lugh did not stand and fight. And if the Ur'Lugh would not fight, why should the rest of the army?

The rats turned and fled.

As Captain Blang's elite unit shredded the Ur'Lugh, the other kingsguard units rushed into battle from the Shade, Open, and Royal gates, converging on the rat center.

Many of the Ur'Lugh were killed. Most fled. The kingsguard then split the rat army down the middle. KoVeek pursued the smaller part westward, toward the now barren cornfield. Captain Blang and his troops drove the larger part of the rat army south through the Dark Forest to the cliffs above the river. There they killed rats for almost an hour as black clouds gathered in the west. Hundreds of rats—shocked at the fury of the kingsguard—threw themselves off the cliffs and were swept away by the river.

"Stop!"

Captain Blang turned and saw JaRed standing in the open space between the trees and the cliff. A few dozen rats huddled near the edge, looking back and forth between the sheer drop to the river and the menacing and revenge-minded kingsguard.

JaRed held up the bloody nail, and the sight of it brought a shudder to rat and mouse alike. "Enough," he said simply.

"But they are getting what they deserve," Captain Blang said. "If we let them live, who knows what will happen?"

"Perhaps," JaRed said. "But if we all get what we deserve, no one will ever be happy." He sighed heavily, and it seemed to Captain Blang that JaRed had grown immensely taller and decades older.

"Is there no room for mercy in your heart, Captain Blang?"

◆ ◆ ◆

The presence JaRed had felt twice before washed over him again. Peace, as tangible as the moisture in the air, rippled across the battlefield.

Captain Blang opened his mouth to speak. Then his shoulders slumped, and he nodded slowly. "All right. Let them go." He turned and walked wearily into the trees, toward home. His face revealed nothing but a mask of hidden sadness. He seemed lost, wounded. He returned no salute, answered no questions, offered no victory cheer.

JaRed ordered the remaining rats be taken captive, and he told KoVeek to treat them with dignity.

The sun had disappeared. Storm clouds roiled overhead in churning waves of black and gray, and the sight of them brought a smile to his face.

JaRed was tired. Bone weary. Next to a long drink of cold water, he wanted nothing so much as to curl up in his own fur-cozy sleeping chambers and sleep for weeks.

But all danger had not passed.

He had seen something shocking in King SoSheth's eyes just before the fight with GoRec. The king was jealous of him. Jealous ... and afraid.

The king wants me dead.

What a strange realization that was. JaRed looked heavenward as rain began to spatter in huge droplets all around him.

How ironic, he thought. *The king of Tira-Nor, the most powerful mouse in the land, is afraid of me ... Runt!*

Chapter Twelve

The House of Men

Tall Grass

Tira-Nor

The Corn Field
here there be snakes

Dry Gully

Round Top

The Dark Forest

N

KNOWN WORLD

Winding Cliffs

The Abandoned Quarry

Horrid

I t took weeks to bury the dead, clean out the tunnels, and rebuild the city's damaged defenses.
The rain that came at the end of what the mice
later called "The Battle of JaRed's Fang" lingered for
days. The city was forced to live on the food they had
saved for the siege. But no one complained.

Eventually the mice of Tira-Nor got around to cele-
brating. A feast was held in the Great Hall. The best of
the reserved berries and nuts and dried crickets were
taken out of reserve, and the social barriers of the past
were, for one evening at least, removed.

The king arrived with a train of supporters and nose-dabbers. YuLooq the merchant waddled in and staked out a corner near a pile of juicy raisins. Kingsguard warriors mingled among the militia. Even TaMir was there.

Only a few members of the Families snubbed the event, preferring instead to attend a private affair in the home of SingleBerry the Nose. "After all," SingleBerry sniffed to a handful of glum-looking aristocracy, "a celebratory feast ought to be held in a place with more dignity, don't you agree? The Commons, no offense to the rabble, is, well, rather pedestrian, what?"

To the surprise of many, King SoSheth showed JaRed no gratitude for killing GoRec, though he did excuse JaRed's father from paying the royal tax for the rest of ReDemec's natural life. This made ReDemec very happy, but caused no end of grumbling among the common mice, who expected some more notable reward for JaRed. "He killed the Great Rat," they whispered. "He killed the serpent. Is there anything JaRed can't do?"

When King SoSheth overheard one such comment, he turned red about the nose, claimed he'd left something important back in the royal palace, and stomped away sulkily on his royal paws.

The stories and songs lasted late into the night — far later than the raisins. Winter, after all, stood not far off, and the king had wisely given orders to keep the flow of food "steady but thin."

Nevertheless, most of the commoners were still in or near the Great Hall just after midnight when TaMir shuffled to the center. He cleared his throat, and a hush descended on the huge chamber. Even the kits listened, for mouse kits love stories and are always quick to understand truth presented as fiction, as well as fiction presented as truth.

TaMir gazed thoughtfully about the room. He understood the heaviness of the feast. He saw sadness in many eyes. He saw loss and grief. He knew why the mice of Tira-Nor needed to celebrate, and why the celebration could not meet their need.

"ElShua," he said through a voice thick with age and emotion, "has given me a vision. Just now, in fact, as I rested here among you."

He turned in a broad circle. A mouseling climbed wearily into his mother's lap, rubbing his eyes to stay awake.

"ElShua's garden blooms." TaMir said. "The Earthpool is large now. It shimmers in the fields of the garden like the night sky, and its depths are filled with many lights. At the edges, wave after wave heaves against the shore, beating its boundaries wider."

His audience did not understand, perhaps, but neither did they interrupt.

"In the pool, souls shine like stars against a black veil, and when the Great Owl plucks a star from the waters and brings it to ElShua's side—behold! A mouse, a snake, a shrew. Sometimes, even a rat."

TaMir paused, waiting for someone to protest, but no one did. He sighed, nodded, pursed his lips. He was looking for the right words, though only adequate ones presented themselves.

"The Great Owl is old and wise and silent, and his flight is graceful. He spreads his wings wide. He turns carefully. He glides as patiently as the moon. His burdens are carried lightly."

RewHenna, widow of MarSihlu the Builder, nodded, as if to say, *Good*. And, *yes*. And, *I had thought so. Hoped so. Prayed so. But even so, it is good to hear. Good to say.*

Don't stop, the nod said.

An older mouse began to weep. *Don't lie to me, seer*, his eyes said. *Don't offer me something I can't accept.*

But it wasn't a lie, and there was no reason not to accept it.

"I saw the Owl land like a cloud before the Maker," TaMir said. "He held a burden in one talon. Held it gently, delicately. Then the Owl folded his wings and lay the burden at ElShua's feet. And he nudged the burden with the blunt hook of his beak, crooning forward like a mother hen."

He paused. "It was a mouse. An older mouse. One of us, certainly. Though I couldn't see the face, I did see the back. It was covered in blood."

The air of the Great Hall hung thick with hope, longing. Someone sniffed. A mother stroked her child's head. More mice appeared at the entrances of the hall, clotted the openings, jammed into a circle all around him. There was a sense that something they had long been looking for was almost found.

TaMir could almost hear their minds spinning. *He didn't see the face! It might have been anyone.*

"Behold." TaMir's voice came as a whisper, yet the words were sharp and unmistakable. "Even as I watched, the mouse stirred! He roused himself, drew life from the air of the garden, and stood. His wounded back … Well. Bloody, But also straight. He stood like a soldier."TaMir gazed into the eyes of the kingsguard, and each one stood tall. "Then ElShua held out His hands, palm up. Like this. An invitation. And I heard the Great Owl say, 'So many of your people dead. When will it end, Lord?' And ElShua replied, 'When all have chosen joy or sorrow.'"

TaMir closed his eyes, willing them to receive the blessing he offered. But did they understand? Did they hear? Could they believe the mouse of TaMir's vision was really their own loved one, their own husband or father or friend? Would they realize the vision was only a foretaste of something that had been repeated since the beginning of time? Would they recognize the Maker's heart in the story, even if the mouse TaMir saw wasn't their own dead, but a certain someone?

He didn't know. Didn't know how to tell them. Didn't know how to end the story.

Mercifully, a kit spoke. "But Master TaMir," the high, squeaking voice said.

TaMir opened his eyes. NuFal, son of FalKirq the Quick gazed up at him. Innocent. Hungry. Pleading. "Who was the mouse you saw in your vision?"

He saw the same question repeated in the eyes of the others. *Was it FalKirq? Was it RuMin?*

Tell us. But don't lie.

TaMir exhaled slowly. He knew who the mouse of the vision was. He had known by the posture, though he had not seen the face. He had recognized the gaudy stance, the quicksilver leap into the Maker's palm.

In his mind, he watched as a broad smile stretched across ElShua's face.

The mouse saluted grandly.

It is, said the mouse, *an honair*.

◆ ◆ ◆

You may wonder how JaRed became king of Tira-Nor. After all, ElShua said he would be king, and everyone knows ElShua does not lie.

But the *how* of JaRed becoming king of Tira-Nor is not to be found in this book (although, if you know where to look, it may be found in another). As TaMir told JaRed, the *how* of life is what makes life interesting, though it always comes in a way you don't expect, and long after you've been told the *what*.

Yet there is one more part of the story to tell here.

One night soon after the feast, but long before JaRed recovered from the loss of his mother, he awoke in his private chambers to the presence of another mouse.

"JaRed," the mouse said.

JaRed blinked. "Horrid?" *Could it be*? His brother had always called him Runt, never by his given name.

But it was true. Horrid knelt just outside his sleeping chamber, trembling. "There is something I must tell you. When Mother died ... her last words ..." He paused as though searching for the right thing to say. "I didn't know what she meant until the day you killed GoRec. But now I do."

JaRed leaned forward. "Tell me," he said. He had not known Mother had thought of him as she died.

"You must promise to listen to everything I say first," Horrid said. There was something in his voice

JaRed had never heard, something that sounded like pain.

"All right."

Slowly, as though feeling his way over unfamiliar ground in the darkness, Horrid spilled the story of how he had betrayed JaRed's anointing to King SoSheth.

"And now it cannot be undone," Horrid concluded. "The king hates and fears you, and it is my fault. And this is what I came to tell you: *I'm sorry*. Instead of helping you, instead of helping my family and my fellow mice, I have only created a more deadly enemy. I do not deserve your kindness or your friendship, JaRed. But will you forgive me anyway?"

Now, I hope you will not think too little of JaRed if I tell you that, for just a moment, he found it very difficult to say, "I forgive you, HaRed." But in the end he did say it, and afterward he realized that it had not been so very hard a thing to say after all. And he found himself thinking, in spite of everything, that he might actually come to like HaRed.

Someday.

The End

Naming of Mice

By tradition, the mice of Tira-Nor take their names from the parent of the same sex. Male children are named for their fathers, females for their mothers. Names are made by combining a new syllable with the first one or two syllables of the parent's name. The new syllable represents identity and distinction; the old represents community and tradition.

Thus were ReDemec's sons all given his identity, Red, in addition to their own: KeeRed, BeRed, MaRed, HaRed, JaRed. ReDemec's lone daughter was named

after her mother, EeShawna, and given her own identity, Kah, which means "life." The name seems to
imply that her ability to bear kits has passed to the
next generation.

Experts believe the naming traditions of Tira-Nor
were intended by TyMin to hinder the building of
powerful family clans, which would weaken the city's
sense of community. However, by the time of the events
of this book, the mice of Tira-Nor were no less political
than those in surrounding colonies.

SoSheth, the first outright king of Tira-Nor,
exempted himself from the tradition by naming his son
JoHanan. He apparently anticipated fathering a stronger, more powerful male and wanted to reserve his own
name for his imagined successor. It was rumored that
he intended to name this would-be second kit SoSheth.

Glossary

The Commons: The largest section of Tira-Nor. Home of the commoners who make up the city's majority. The Commons is the shallowest level of the city, the section closest to the surface. In recent years it expanded downward as the population of the city increased and the need for additional chambers grew more urgent.

ElShua: The soft-spoken Creator. The Maker of the universe and Ruler of all living things. The name literally means "who whispers," indicating that the Creator speaks quietly and with great significance. To a mouse, a whispered message is more important than a shouted one. But the greater implication of "who whispers" is that of nearness. Since a whisper cannot be heard from far off, ElShua must be close at hand. A more complete and accurate translation might be "He who is so close He need only whisper to be heard."

The Families: A section of Tira-Nor reserved for the upper class.

Gate: An entrance into, or exit from, Tira-Nor. A hole in the ground protected on the inside by a series of guard chambers and booby traps. The twelve gates of Tira-Nor are named for their locations around the city. Because Tira-Nor is a city of multiple layers, its gates vary in depth, size, and complexity.

Glowstone: A phosphorescent rock used by the mice of Tira-Nor to light the tunnels and chambers of their underground city.

The Great Owl: Death. To mice, he is an agent of ElShua, though one greatly feared. It is significant that mice see death as a nocturnal predator shrouded in mystery. The Great Owl comes in darkness, unseen and unheard. He is rarely anticipated. A vast number of conflicting myths and fables surround the Great Owl. Some mice, most notably the seers, claim that a literal spirit being—swooping on outstretched wings as white as snow—descends to bear the souls of the dead to eternity.

The kingsguard: The personal bodyguards of the king of Tira-Nor, and the elite fighting force of the city. Also, the section of Tira-Nor that houses the kings-guard warriors. This section of the city encompasses and connects all others, somewhat like the hub of a wheel. From the kingsguard level of Tira-Nor, it is possible to get to any of the other sections.

Lord Wroth: The god of the rats, prairie dogs, weasels, and possums. Many mice believe Lord Wroth to be a real spirit being, while others say the power of the legend of Lord Wroth lies in the fact that the rats believe it. Rat theology describes a great number of different gods acting in various ways with different forms of life. Thus the rats worship Lord Wroth, the mice of Tira-Nor follow ElShua, the mice of Cadrid follow Kalla, the white mice of Leer and the serpents of the Known Lands serve SeeEqueq. Although the rats seem to comprehend the mouse ideal of a single Creator, they greatly resent it—possibly because they believe it to be true, but don't want it to be.

Militia: Volunteers and conscripts. Mice who are unaccustomed to the disciplined life of a soldier are, in times of dire need, taken into civilian military service to defend the city. The militia is usually commanded by two or three officers of the kingsguard.

SoSheth: The first king of Tira-Nor, anointed by TaMir some twelve seasons before the events of this book. TaMir later revoked the blessing of ElShua he had previously given to SoSheth, and from that point on SoSheth never esteemed TaMir, nor the God TaMir claimed to serve. It was also at this point that SoSheth began to act strangely, and many in his service noticed that he became volatile, short tempered, and unpredictable.

TaMir: The seer who anointed SoSheth—and later JaRed—king over Tira-Nor. Marked from birth as a seer by his all-white fur, TaMir was dedicated to ElShua by his mother and trained under RuHoff.

Tira-Nor: Literally, "the city of promise." Generations earlier, according to stories handed down by the elders, ElShua drove the ancient prairie dogs from the city and gave it to the followers of the mouse TyMin, founder of Tira-Nor.

The Ur'Lugh: The personal bodyguard of GoRec, king of the rats. Most of the Ur'Lugh were destroyed in the Battle of JaRed's Fang, as it came to be known later.